the virtues of Joy

~ compilation of short stories ~

Joycelyn Wells

the virtues of Joy

~compilation of short stories~

S.H.A.P.E.

Self, Health &
Personal Empowerment
www.aboutshape.com

To My Trio,

Joya Danielle. Jasmine Denese. Quintin Ananias.

I could not have imagined a more perfect three.

Table of Contents

Acknowledgements

*a thing done or given in recognition of
something received*

God. Knows.

My Light. You love me, just as I am. What a daunting task! Thoughts of you constantly flow through my mind; I often wonder what it would feel like to write you. You know? How would the words of you feel flowing from my mind to my fingertips to the pages in front of me? How would you look in print? How would your mind respond to seeing you as I do? Could I get my readers to feel for you, what I feel when I think of you? How amazing would that be for every person to feel like I feel with you, My Light, inside? You will have my love forever. #everything

My Dawn. There are so many reasons for me to be grateful. You believed in this project, as much as I. Thank you for eagerly reading every word. Thank you for coming up with an amazing title. I'll never be able to thank you enough for creating such a beautiful piece of artwork. Lastly, for being my friend and loving me unconditionally, I will always be grateful.

Mom.

Dad.

Preface

the introductory remarks of a speaker or author

Prior to transferring these stories from my mind to my fingers to the pages of this book, I would constantly create and recite stories aloud in my head. I refer to it as reciting and not just thinking because the story teller sometimes speaks louder than the thought maker. Yes, unfortunately, there is always a party in my brain. Well, maybe not so unfortunate, I was able to write this book of short stories. Hilarious! For me, inspiration was and is still found any and everywhere. I have millions of stories tucked away. When I was younger, I didn't understand why others couldn't see what I saw or think what I thought. As we all know, people have a tendency to make you believe that something is wrong with you when your thoughts differ from theirs. Though, amazingly every book I ever read understood me, as I understood it. Therefore, books became my comfort, my source of mutual understanding.

Years ago, I remember calling my Uncle William. I was upset. He's always calm. He taught me to be calm. To breathe, listen for the facts, and then repeat the facts before responding with my own assessment. He's methodical, as well. He said, "What's going on Gnat?" He gave me that nickname as a little girl. Anyway, I began, patiently and calmly, giving him the backstory which lead to my explaining how I felt as if I were different from everyone around me. I continued telling him that I felt like I was interacting with the crowd from the outside. It's like I'm a part of the crowd but they don't understand me when I interject. He listened. Finally, it was his turn to talk. I was expecting possibly a suggestion to see a therapist or the worse, an agreement of my self-assessment. He just said, "Gnat, you are fine." He delivered this statement as a fact then there was silence. I couldn't question his comment. I believed him. Besides, I didn't know anything other than to trust his words. He has always been the truth in my life.

In our moment of silence, events from his life, flashed vividly in my mind. It was then I realized he was different too. That's why he knew that I was fine. He recognized my words as his own from a time long gone. Calm settled my mind and spirit. William began to talk again. He told me that we are all different. Many of us are incapable of simulating, that's what makes the difference. He talked through his thought. I listened. His goal was to reinforce my positive sense of being. He was successful. To this day, he is still the person I call when I'm caught in the trap of my own mind. Fortunately for both of us, at this age, the calls are less frequent but just as important. Even to this day, the final piece of advice he shared continues to hold true... "always try to do the right thing." He went on to say, if the right thing is the goal, it's difficult to be questioned about your intentions or to even question your own. He was absolutely right.

This compilation of short stories, *The Virtues of Joy*, began as a single journal entry about two years ago. Though, the idea of a book manifested during a car ride through the Georgia Mountains. I shared the partially written story with two of my friends over the same weekend. While reading to my best girlfriend after her surgery, she said "J that's amazing!" Then she fell asleep. So, I wasn't sure if she really enjoyed it or if her medications were speaking for her. Too funny! When I was reading to my guy friend as he was driving, he interrupted the reading. He reached for my hand and said, with such seriousness "is that you? Did you write that?" I started laughing and replied, "Wait, you can't interrupt the story, Jeez, let me finish." When I stopped reading he said "now, that is my new favorite author. Is that you? Did you write that?" I replied "yes, how did you know?" He said that he recognized a couple of the 'true Joy' phrases. I laughed. He asked, "Will you read more?" I started to blush because he wanted more but there wasn't anymore. He told me that I should finish writing the story. Voila! Just like that, I promised myself that I would complete the story for the sole purpose of sharing with him.

After completing the story, I was extremely proud. I read and reread my words as if they belonged to someone else. I honestly couldn't believe that those words flowed from within me. I was like "God? Seriously? Is this what we are about to do?" He responded with more stories. The words continued to flow; I kept writing, story after story. At some point, the idea of connecting each story to a virtue came to the forefront of my brain. I told another of my good girlfriends about the virtues idea. As I explained it to her, it didn't even make sense to me but I realized that it was a part of the gift, my gift. She, in fact, came up with the title... *The Virtues of Joy*. Now, the book is here, it's a reality. You have it in your hands.

Living by the virtues is like a constant reminder that love and compassion exists for all humanity. They keep me focused on doing what I believe to be right in that moment. Have you ever explored the virtues of life? Of course, there are many, but these first 10 arrived for *The Virtues of Joy*, literally, with a bow. As a woman, I have always tried to maintain a balance of my sexuality and social expectations. My mother began teaching me 'how to be a lady' from the moment I was born. Though, as for my sexual self, it was discovered at a very young age, maybe 6, through books, of course. The beauty of discovering sex through books is that you develop an elevated sense of your sexual self, prior to someone else experimenting or experiencing you. Now, that has proven to be, an amazing life-long gift.

I have noticed, when I'm writing, the party in my brain ceases. The story teller, the thought maker, the imagination and the balance keeper all calm the fuck down, literally. It's seems as if they are all waiting patiently to find out what will happen next. Wait! Are they waiting to find out or are they working diligently together to write what's happening next? Hmm I'll have to think about that at a later time. Writing has proven to be a most awesome outlet for me. I cannot wish to have found it sooner because I wouldn't have been in a place to receive his gift. God's timing was perfect and I was prepared.

Also, while writing I've noticed that my mind and body are in complete harmony. My body stands at attention. It wants to relive and experience every sensation developed by the words flowing through my fingers. Amazingly, as I reread the stories, I can still laugh, roll my eyes in exasperation and feel my body tighten in preparation for a kiss or a touch. Even as I reread the words each of the experiences present as brand new. I hope that you, the reader, will find pleasure as you experience *The Virtues of Joy...*

March 20, 2017

And beside this, giving all diligence,
add to your faith virtue,
and to your virtue knowledge.
--- 2 Peter 1:5 (KJV)

Virtue

particular moral excellence

I will also clothe her priests with salvation;
and her saints shall shout aloud for joy.
---Psalms 132:16 (KJV)

Joy

the emotion evoked by well-being, success
or good fortune or by the prospect of
possessing what one desires

the virtues of Joy

~ compilation of short stories ~

Courage

mental or moral strength to venture, persevere, and withstand danger, fear, or difficulty

Tabitha and I were sitting at the bar chatting it up with some folks. It was our usual M.O. after work on Fridays. This particular Friday was different because we wanted to hit a couple of spots that required club attire. So, we went home right after work and met back up at 7. So, now we are here! I'm sitting on a bar stool facing the bar, Tabitha is next to me, sitting but facing away from the bar. Of course, there's a very handsome gentleman standing with us, keeping us engaged and making us laugh. I can't even remember what we were talking about; it probably wasn't relevant anyway. We order another round of drinks while we continue chatting, laughing and chair dancing to the DJ spinning the tracks.

After a few minutes, I motioned to Tabitha using my right hand to watch my seat, I've gotta go to the ladies' room. As she's grooving to the music, she winks and nods ok. So, I'm out. I scoot off my stool and sashay to ladies' room. Yeah, I was looking hot. I was feeling myself. I entered the ladies room, made use of the facilities, washed my hands, reapplied my lipstick and then kinda danced-walked back to my spot at the bar. Overall, it was a pretty regular night.

Something I have noticed about myself is that in a crowd of people I rarely notice any faces. I'm in a zone. I wonder if other people have the same experience. When I got back to my seat, the guy who was chatting with us was sitting down. We can call him Jay. Well, he starts to rise; I shake my head and tell him "no, go ahead, I want to dance a bit." He continued to sit. I danced in place for a few songs, talked to a few different people approaching the bar. After a while, Jay acknowledges someone approaching, he stood up and offered me the stool. I accepted. So, Jay and I switched places. He introduced us to the newcomer, one of his boys. Now, there are four of us talking. From the outside looking in, we probably looked as if we were a couple of couples. Honestly, at the time, I didn't even think about it.

18

Reader, keep in mind, I'm sitting facing the bar so my back is to the crowd. I'm totally relaxed, chilling, sipping on my drink and still...chair dancing, AYE! All of a sudden, my fucking stool starts to move. At first I thought, someone bumped me, but as I tried to turn to see what happened, I realized that I was being lifted off the fucking ground still sitting on my fucking stool. I looked at Tabitha; she looked surprised and has her hand covering her mouth like "oh shit." I'm too terrified to turn around because I might lose my balance and fall.

It took my mind a split second to realize that someone was purposefully transporting me, and my stool, to another area of the bar. People were watching but no one was coming to my rescue, I just shook my head and was like what the fuck is going on. By now, Tabitha is laughing her ass off. The men who were talking with us were just watching, everyone was trying to figure it out. After 10ft or so, the moving stopped; I was lowered to the ground with great care. I'm usually pretty controlled; it's my nature, so I had to get it together before I faced my abductor. I didn't turn around. I just sat. I mean, hell, if he were bold enough to move me, he should be bold enough to face me, right? Several minutes passed, I sat...waiting. No one approached me; no one said a single word to me. Out of curiosity some of the bar crowd continued looking; others went on with their evening.

I'll admit, once I processed the worse possible scenario, I was quite amused. Seriously, I was in the middle of a freaking bar with a crowd of people watching. What's going to happen? The energy was calm, music was filling the room, and people were watching and laughing, including my girl. I'd like to think that I would've been aware of a strange man, or any man, coming to harm me. Right?

Finally, he showed his face. He came from behind me on my left side. I'm still looking forward but I saw him moving out of the corner of my eye. I knew it was him because no one dared get this close or interfere in this moment. He didn't say anything; he walked in front of me and then turned to face me. We made eye contact. I remember rubbing my tongue across my lips, just slightly. Maybe I was making sure that my mouth was functional, just in case, I had to curse this motherfucker out. I'm not sure of the expression on my face but I am sure some level of annoyed curiosity was reflected. I continued to wait. I was not giving him an easy out. He was going to have to follow through with his plan.

He cleared his throat and spoke, "Hello, I'm James."

I looked. He took a deep breath. I waited.

"I brought you a drink."

I continued to look at this well-dressed man with the social skills of a caveman. Though, now, I'm looking on purpose. James is handsome, possibly 5'10 or so. His features are bold. His look is of focus and determination. He hasn't smiled... yet. Just like that, my curiosity turned to intrigue.

"Good evening James. How may I help you?"

I didn't reach for the drink. My hands are together resting on my lap.

James replied, "I wanted to talk to you."

"Well James, you could have come over to say "hello."

20

He continued to look at me or maybe he was looking into me. He was shifting his weight from one foot to the other. Wait, he appears to be nervous. Hmph it was a bit too late for that.

He said, "I've been watching you all night. I was tired of waiting."

I inhale deeply which caused me to sit higher and straighter. On exhale, I asked "tired of waiting for what?"

He gave a slight smile, causing his eyes to sparkle, and then said "for those guys to leave you alone for one moment. Now, which one is coming for you?"

I smiled inside and thought, he's trying to gauge the level of chaos which his actions may have triggered.

He continued, "and as I said before, I wanted to talk to you."

"Well, lucky for both of us, no one is coming for me." I smiled and my eyes softened, "Now James, don't you think this approach was a tad bit dramatic?"

He maintained eye contact and asked, "Do I have your attention?"

With a laugh and a shake of my head, I answered, "yes, yes you have my attention."

With a bigger smile, he said, "Good, then it worked. I have a drink for you."

With that we laughed, I stuck out my right hand for a handshake; he reached out to take my hand but instead of a handshake, he kissed the back and laughed. Lord, after all this, this n-word is trying to be gallant and kind. Dramatic much? I introduced myself, "Good evening James, I'm Joy." After the hand kiss, he held up the drink that he'd been holding this whole time. I received it, held it up to an imaginary toast, "Cheers to cavemen everywhere" and took a sip. We laughed and relaxed more. As we talked, the onlookers kinda laughed, walked away and lost interest. Tabitha looked over to get a thumb up that everything was cool. I smiled, rolled my eyes and nodded my head, signaling that I was good. She and I would talk on the way to venue #2. "Cause we making moves tonight!"

James and I continued to chat for a few moments. Random topics, of course, where are you from? Do you come here often? Blah, blah, blah...

After a couple of drinks and dances, I was bold enough to revisit the abduction. "James?" I was dancing in front of him. "Yes?' he said. I stopped dancing and asked with a smile and slow dramatic pauses between words, kinda a mix of anger and humor "What the fuck were you thinking picking me up that way? It was crazy!" He stopped dancing and replied, "That wasn't as dramatic as I wanted." I leaned in 'really astonished' "what did you WANT to do?" Because I couldn't think of anything more dramatic.

He looked at me deep into my eyes, as if trying to decide if he was going to say what the hell ever he was thinking or, if he were anchoring to gauge a reaction when he gives his response. I couldn't tell, but one thing is for sure, he had my attention. He began, "I wanted to pick you up, put you over my shoulder, carry you outside and fuck you in my car."

I can assure you my heart skipped a beat. An electric shock went from my ears to my brain to my orgasm control center. My body started to heat up from the center out to the extremities. Fuck! Impulsively, my thighs squeezed together. Why in the hell was that such a turn on?

22

My hands were beginning to moisten. I had to close my mouth to hold my saliva. My nipples shifted against my bra. Breathe, breathe. It took me a moment to respond because I was lost in the savagery of his comment. Me? Seriously? Could I incite this kind of desire in a man? This whole time I'm having a conversation in my mind, he knew it too. He wasn't trying to read my mind, he was focused on my carnal response. He would not release my eyes from his captive. Yes, he was a caveman and I, unbeknownst to me, was a cavewoman. As witty and clever as I normally am, can you believe the only reply my silly ass could come up with was "what if I said no?"

This man of men in all his boldness, took my drink from my hand, turned from me, walked to a table and placed it there. I just stood, I didn't move. I watched him as he walked back. No hurries. No worries. He leaned in, placed his mouth close to my ear, so close, in fact, that I could feel his words vibrate as he whispered, "Joy, I didn't ask." I had to force myself to swallow; my brain was preparing my body for him without talking to my mind. Traitor! Slowly, he leaned back, watching me, searching for his answers to "will she come willingly?" or "am I about to catch a charge?" I couldn't move. I inhaled, swallowed, exhaled, as quietly as possible, and then my eyes lowered. He recognized my surrender. He stood up, then bent his knees slightly, wrapped his right arm around my back, his left arm around my knees, stood up, lifted me onto his shoulder, like a fucking sack of potatoes and carried me outside. Holy shit! What was even crazier is that at this moment it seemed so natural. He saw, wanted and took with minimal social interactions. I obliged. I wasn't aware that I had of a choice. We were cave people!

As we were leaving, of course, we passed by several people, they were looking, laughing and making comments. I started giggling and even shrugged my shoulders in response. Well, now my mind is becoming conscious again, and I could feel myself tense up against this caveman.

Obviously, James felt it too, because he took this moment to reach up and rub my back with a firm yet gentle hand. He's calming me. His touch was reassurance that everything is fine. I relaxed. Focused and determined to see this mission through. James continued walking. We haven't spoken a single word, since we exited the bar. It seems like we walked for a long time, but probably not. I don't think time exists in this pre-historic space.

He stops. I can feel him searching, reaching for his keys. Chirp, chirp. Doors unlock. No words. I can feel him lowering me to the ground. Our eyes met, I notice that his breathing is heavier, faster. His eyes are black holes of heat. I'm burning up in them. He reached up with his hand, not sure left or right, and grabbed the base of my neck. At this point, he could've done anything, I belonged to him. With his other hand, he unbuttoned my dress, every single button, all while holding me in place by my neck. I'm sure he could feel me quivering, shaking and trying to control my breathing. Now, my dress is open, he leans down and bites my breast through my bra. Fuck it I released a moan. I was holding on to it for too long anyway. He bent down and kissed my stomach a couple of times, then reached for my panties. I shifted slightly to open my legs, to allow him access. He placed his face to the crotch of my panties. My heat drew him in. At which time, he lowered himself to one knee then the other. He allows his face to get closer and linger, no movement, just inhalations and exhalations. I feel myself getting hotter. I'm not sure how long my legs can hold. I moved my hand to find something to use as a brace when I realized that we were still outside of his car, truck, tractor or whatever the fuck it was.

James stood up, still maintaining his hold on my neck, maybe he was keeping me from running or maybe he was holding on to his newest conquest. Either way the heat from his hand became one with my neck. It belonged there. I belonged here. He opened the back door

24

driver's side. No words. He lifted and moved me onto the edge of backseat. I sat there. He reached for something... knife, club, rope or condom? I was secretly hoping for the later. He applied gentle pressure to my chest to prompt me to lie down. I followed his unspoken request. Now, I'm lying down, focused on the interior light of the car because I'm naked in the parking lot of a bar with a caveman. I can feel him trying to remove my panties. I lift my hips up, panties, down, off. He then lifts my legs, bending them up on the seat so that my knees are in the air; the heels of my shoes pressed into the seat. I'm still focused on the light. James rubs his face on my thighs. He begins to nibble and taste and lick. Nibble and taste and lick. Nibble and taste and lick until my hips started rocking back and forth into his face forcing him to drink from my sweetness. He was not in any hurry. I'm sure he could've held me in this position for hours but as nature would have it the cabin light gradually turned to darkness and the fireworks began to light the night. I'm lying there, knees relaxed into the open position, as the light became visible again, I could hear the sounds of James' licking. I supposed he was trying to take as much of his prize with him as possible.

Still no words, he reached into the back seat, I took his hand. He pulled me to a sitting position. He captured my eyes, grabbed me by the hips, and pulled me out of the car to a standing position. I tried to make sure my legs were functional. He wouldn't allow movement. With his hands on my hips, he began to turn me around. Once I was facing the car, submitting as any good cavewoman would, he applied pressure to my upper back to bend me over. I followed this order too. Bent over, face down on the back seat, I can hear the paper tear from the condom. I listened to the process of him putting it on. I can feel his hand on my shoulder and the back of my neck, instinctively, my back arches. He reached under my ass with his hand. I can feel his dick searching, seeking looking for a place to bury itself. Aaaaahhh, mmmm, that's it, right there, pressure, entry, more pressure, breathe. James is now on autopilot; this isn't about me anymore. He's holding me tight at my shoulder and my hip; he is focused on releasing whatever he felt when he started this mission. His action was brutal, hard, forceful, carnal, pleasurable and intoxicating. We were both lost in it. James was finally saying something but I'm sure he wasn't aware of the guttural sounds leaving his body. He reached around and under my hip to rub my clitoris which ignited more fireworks for me. His hip movements increased. Stronger, harder, and deeper and finally he could see the fireworks. We both lay there; him on top of me until he regained his sense of being.

Gradually, he started moving. I continued to lay there while he fixed his clothes. When he was done, he put his hands on my hips to pull me out of the car. He turned me around to face him. He touched my face gently, pulled my bra down to cover my breast, and then one button at a time closed my dress.

Aloud, I had a thought, "where are my panties?" It was then James asked his only question of the night, "May I please have them?" I looked him in the eyes; we stayed in that moment for a few seconds. I replied, "Yes, of course" with a slight smile. He thanked me as he closed the door to car. Chirp, chirp. Door locked.

Well James, with all of his dramatics, scooped me back up over his shoulders and retraced his steps back inside the bar. At which point, he delivered me safely back to my girl, Tabitha, who was still chair dancing, drinking and chilling at the bar! I smiled at James. He said that it was a pleasure meeting me. I agreed. We hugged good-bye. He turned and walked away.

Tabitha and I were talking and laughing. I was trying to fill her in on all the dirty details. We decided that it was about time for us to make our next move; However, a few moments later, the server showed up with another round of drinks. We both said, "We didn't order drinks" and laughed. I scanned the crowd trying to see from where the drinks came. There he was, the Caveman with a smile, holding my panties to his nose, lifting his head to signal goodbye. I smiled and waved, "Goodbye James, The Keeper of the Fire."

Perseverance

continued effort to do or achieve something despite difficulties, failure, or opposition

I've been invited to a birthday party at a hotel not far from my home. Perfect! I can drink and party close to home. Now, that is truly the set up for the best night ever. If I remember correctly, it was a black and white party, maybe it wasn't. Hell, I don't know. I do know there was some kind of theme or gimmick, most parties now- a -days have a theme; nevertheless, I wore black and white. At the time, I was the proud owner of some boot cut white slacks. They were fabulous. I wore those and a black and white off the shoulder blouse. Whenever I wore those pants, I knew my ass was looking amazing! I loved the white pants season!

I went to the party by myself. I was not worried. I'll know plenty of people there. Besides, I go places by myself all the time. That's the single life! The party is being held in a penthouse suite overlooking the pool. When I entered the suite, I was like "Damn this is my home. I could live here." The food was yummy, music was hot and drinks were flowing. As parties go, lots of great conversations and squeals of excitement. The birthday girl was totally turned up. We danced all the hustles and to everything Mary J.

At some point, in the evening, three gentlemen entered, nice looking, I might add. I noticed they were just standing around, not talking or drinking or dancing. So, I sauntered, by this time my heels were off because I was relaxed, up to them, introduced myself, "Hi, I'm Joy" and asked if they would like a drink. Two of them were like, "Yeah, that would be cool." Playing a great hostess fill-in, I took their orders... beer and rum with coke. I left to fill the order and find the true hostess. Well, the hostess was in the bathroom playing grown up bathroom games. With that revelation, I entered the kitchen area to fill the orders for the handsome men. I grabbed a Corona, placed it on the counter, opened it, inserted a lime slice and then proceeded to make rum with just a splash of coke. Ha! Loosen up Dude! I head back to the gentlemen with drinks in tow. I held up the Corona and said "Corona" because I didn't know who wanted what; I wasn't paying that much attention. Then I lifted the glass that held the rum and coke, the middle guy took it. We chatted for a moment. I asked if they needed anything else, they said that they were good. Cool. I left them standing there while I went to the dance area.

I noticed that Gentleman #3, no drink, kept watching me, which was weird because when I was in his face he was silent. Oh, well, whatever, men are always drawn to my energy, if he wants to talk to me, he will. So I danced a couple of more songs. As the song ended, I noticed #3 watching me, yet again. So, I went to him and said "I'm sorry; I didn't get your name." He said, "Torrance." "Hi Torrance would you like to dance?" He replied, "I don't dance." I shrugged my shoulders, "oh ok, just checking.' So, I got a little jazzy 'cause I was buzzing. I continued, "Let me see, you don't talk, drink or dance. What do you do?" He laughed and started explaining how his boys told him that he works too much and convinced him to come to this party to let his hair down. Figuratively speaking, I guessed, because he was bald. I nodded and said something like "sounds good. What line of work are you in?" He replied "I'm a high school principal." I threw my head back and laughed, "They are absolutely right, you do work too much!" I went on to add that I was high school science teacher.

And that is how Torrance and I became instant buddies. We must have talked for an hour easy. When the hostess reappeared she mentioned that there were some people going to the pool area to smoke cigars, say no more... pool area and cigars, I was with it. I smiled and asked Torrance "are you coming down?" Of course, he said, "I don't smoke or swim." I rolled my eyes and laughed, "Jeez you are boring as fuck. Come on, you CAN sit and watch, can't you?" He smiled and followed. On the way out of the suite, I refreshed my drink and grabbed a bottle of water for Torrance. We headed to the elevator.

31

Once downstairs, I swear he posted up in a chair FARRR away from the pool. I thought he's trying to stay dry in his fancy white linen outfit. I laughed to myself and devilishly thought of ways to get him wet. Well, whatever, I handed Torrance his bottle of water and went over to the smoking area. I chatted with some folks over there, tasted a couple of cigars and sipped my drink. Well, it didn't take long for me to head over to the pool area. I was standing on the edge of the pool thinking of the best way to undress without people realizing that I'm naked when I get into the pool. I noticed a guy that I knew from grade school, chilling on a lounge chair, shirtless. I walked over and said "hey, do you mind if I swim in your shirt?" He asked "what are you gonna have on under it?" I laughed and said "nothing, duh! I'm getting in the pool!" He handed me his shirt and said, "hell yeah, here." I took it. Now, considering my audience, I decided against undressing in front of everyone at the pool. Don't get me wrong, I was surely considering it. Especially, since the pool looked so inviting and I had to pee so badly!

Well, instead, I headed to the ladies' room. I walked by Torrance, he's chilling. His boys have joined him, pulled up chairs and were sitting just as far away as he was. My passing thought, these three clowns. As I shook my head, I had another thought... hmph... "Hey Torrance, will you come with me to the ladies' room? I need to pee and change clothes for the pool." He replied dryly, "You need me for that?" "Well, honestly, I just want a watcher and a...wiper. But that's ok; I'll take care of it." So, off I went to get ready for the pool. I was undressing and rushing to the toilet when I heard a knock at the door. I said aloud "occupied, just a minute." His reply, "Torrance." I smiled. He is so dry. I covered my front by holding my pants in my hand at the center of me. I opened the door. He entered. I was rambling about nothing, I'm sure. He was standing there watching me. I sat on the toilet to finally pee. Once the stream began, relief washed over me. It's hard to pee in front of a stranger! It felt like I peed forever. Torrance didn't utter a single word. However, he did reach over to the roll of toilet tissue. As he unrolled the tissue, he gently folded the squares into rectangles. Now, I watched. When he finished, he stood there with his hand-made rectangle-drying swab. He held it like it was important to him. He's cool. But my mind is fussing at itself for asking for such a request. I guess I thought he wouldn't come or would say no but here he is. My last thought before he spoke, "Damn, how long am I gonna pee?" The last couple of drops rolled down my labia and hit the toilet. Done.

Torrance looked at me and asked, "Is that it?" I laughed and said "yes." So, now, how is this gonna work? He's a pretty tall guy. It would make more sense for me to stand up and open wide but then I may drip on the floor or down my leg. I'm having this internal discussion when Torrance walks toward me and stops. I'm still sitting; he leans over to brace his left arm on the back of the toilet. He is so close to me I can feel his shirt brush against my face and smell his cologne, "oh my good goodness, he smells delicious." I felt light headed. With his right hand he reaches down between my legs, I spread them open wider. I don't know where he's looking but my eyes are closed. I'm bracing myself for this drying. I'm inhaling his fragrance and feeling the heat radiating from his body. Not purposefully the tissue swab brushes my clitoris, I feel a shock of what felt like electricity. I manage to say "front to back." He stopped and said "what?" "Only wipe front to back," I repeated. He said "oh, ok hmm," like he was thinking about it. At this time, he takes the tissue and firmly places it against my vulva and clitoris, he held it there for just a few seconds, I held my breath. Then he proceeded to pat the area dry, moving slightly forward and back, I could feel the air on my clit when he lowered the tissue to move it forward again to avoid the wiping action. This was fucking erotic. Get it together chick. Just like that, he dropped the rectangle swab in the toilet and flushed. The sound prompted my eyes to open. I started breathing again.

Torrance leaned up against the door but said nothing. I was looking at him like "what?" But he was waiting, waiting for me. He's waiting to watch me get dressed for the pool. He is a man of very few words. What the fuck is his deal? Oh, well, I started this shit, so since my pants were already off and I wasn't wearing any panties. I proceeded to remove my blouse, no bra. I folded my clothes, placed them on the back of the toilet in the same place where the borrowed shirt was laying. The short-sleeved shirt had buttons up the front. I slipped my arms in the shirt and turned to face Torrance at the door. I tied the shirttails but made sure it was long enough to cover my cooch area. He reached out and started buttoning from the top. He skipped the first three and buttoned the second three, the others were lost in the knot of the shirt tails. I checked the mirror. Thanked Torrance and we left the bathroom.

As we exited the hotel bathroom to go back to join the others at the pool area, we didn't say anything to each other. Once outside, I kept walking and Torrance joined his boys in their far away chairs. I found a safe, dry place to put my clothes then proceeded to get in the pool. I love to swim. If there is a pool, I need to know beforehand so that I can bring a swimsuit otherwise my naked ass will probably be on display. There were several people in the pool. We laughed, talked and someone made a drink run. Every so often, Torrance and I would make eye contact. At one point, he motioned for me to come over. I laughed and shook my head no and said, "You come to me, I'm all wet and it's warm in here." He thought about it, stood up and began to walk over. At the edge of the pool, I'm looking up at him, he kneels down and asks "Are you having a good time?" Of course, I laughed and said, "oh my gosh yes, the best time ever!" He said, "it looks like it. Why didn't you come over?" I replied, "Well this water feels so good and I didn't want to get you wet in your 'fancy' outfit." We laughed and then he looked at me and said, "Maybe I want you to get me wet." I focused my eyes 'really' now?" Was that a smile? I was looking in his face checking for some indication of what he had going on in that mind of his. So, in true Joy fashion, I followed up with "Hmph, I'll see what I can come up with. I just might get you wet Torrance." I turned and swam off to the center of the pool. He went back to his seat.

I picked up my drink from poolside and realized that I only have two or three more sips before I'll need a refill. I'll get Torrance to get me a drink, if I can move him out of the boring section... snooze! I got out of the pool; walked over to where they were sitting. They were all watching, I figured Torrance must have told them that we had a thing going on... or about our bathroom exploits. I greeted everyone and said directly to Torrance "You ready to get wet?" He just looked at me. He didn't nod or say anything. Fuck it. I took a swig of my drink into my mouth and held it there. I proceeded to walk to closer to him. I was dripping wet from the pool. He leaned back in his chair, causing his legs to separate or making room for my wetness, either one. I kept moving closer. He's leaned back, his head is tilted and looking up at me. I put each hand on each of his legs with my eyes never leaving his face. Now, we are face to face, I go in like I'm gonna kiss him, he exhaled which caused his lips to part, at that time, I placed my sealed lips on his. Then I opened them ever so slightly allowing my cocktail saliva mix to flow slowly in his mouth. He didn't move. He just kept watching me. His eyes closed and then I heard him swallow. I held that position for a few seconds. I removed my lips from his and asked "Are you wet enough?" He didn't say a word but one of his boys was like "Shit, I'm next! Wet me!" We laughed and I asked Torrance "Will you please refill my drink?" He took my glass. I said "1/2 vodka and 1/2 tonic or cranberry." Then I walked back to the pool to resume my playtime.

A few minutes later, here comes the quiet sexy one with my cocktail in his hand. He leaned down, placed my drink poolside and waited for me to swim over. I smiled "Thank you Sir. I'm appreciative." He said, "You are welcome. What time are you leaving?" Now that caught me off guard. Startled "not sure. What's up?" He was straight forward "I'd like to call you." "Oh" I said, "let me give you my number." He pulled out his phone and entered my number as I gave it to him. "Is there a good time to call?" he followed up. I said nonchalantly, "call me whenever, I'm single." He said "cool." Well he went back to his seat. I went on about my frolicking.

Eventually, I realized that I had drank too much to be in the pool, driving or any fucking thing else. So, I exited the pool. I went into the same bathroom to dry off with a pool towel and to change into my dry clothes. I dried my hair with the towel and shook my head in the mirror. I'm always into some mess. I laughed at myself. I had to make my rounds in the penthouse to say goodbye, give hugs and kisses to the birthday girl. As I was doing so, I realized that Torrance and his crew were gone. Hmm admittedly, I was slightly deflated. Oh well, I guess I have tortured him enough for one night. He was a good sport.

I grabbed my purse, keys, shoes and headed to my car. Once in the car, I said a prayer, "Lord keep me safe. I'll be home in a jiffy. Amen." I started my car, secured my seat belt and shifted to drive. It's time to go home. I was going over the events of the night, laughing to myself about myself. I can be a mess... My phone rings. It's late as hell, maybe I left something at the party, I didn't recognize the number. I answered:

Me: "Hello."

Him: "I thought you said you lived close."

Me: "Huh?"

As I said "huh?" I saw headlights flashing on, off, on in my rearview mirror.

Me: "Are you following me?"

Then I turned my blinker on. He turned his blinker on.

Me: Well alright. "We will be there in a second."

I disconnected the call.

I'm caught between panic and yes I'm having sex tonight! I wasn't necessarily concerned about the condition of my place. It's always clean and ready, mainly for me. I couldn't remember if I had any condoms or wine or anything. What am I thinking? I don't need anything else to drink. He's coming to fuck me. I don't have to entertain him. That was the most calming of all of my thoughts, probably because it was the most rational.

I parked. He parked. I didn't say anything. He followed me up the stairs into my apartment. I kicked off my shoes at the door. I didn't turn on a single light. In fact, as I was walking down the hall, I was taking off my blouse. I wasn't freshening up, washing anything, nothing. This is exactly how I am serving this pussy tonight with salt water additives, thanks to the pool. He wasn't fumbling around in the dark; I could hear him moving behind me down the hall. He was following my scent. As I entered the bedroom, I turned toward the door and started removing my pants. Once my pants were removed, I laid on my bed to watch my prey. I'm watching his moves in the darkness. He knows I'm naked, he knows I'm ready. I'm wondering at what point in the evening did I grab his attention. That's irrelevant. He's here because I wanted him.

He's naked. He's moving towards the bed. I lift my head, I wanted my lips to meet his dick. He stopped. I grabbed his dick. Deep breath. I open my mouth to insert his dick. It's warm and salty, I lick and taste my lips, pre-cum? Lovely. The blowjob was good but Torrance wanted to eat me. He pulled back and then flipped me over on my back. He re-inserted his dick in my mouth and then laid down to allow his feast to begin. Now, I really don't have any control over how much dick he's putting in my throat. My mind is caught up in the pleasure but I have to concentrate on not choking to death. Stay focused.

I believe that I had one orgasm like this but I know I had one when I slid down his shaft for a fabulous fucking ride. My hips were sliding and gliding back and forth allowing my g-spot house to grind into him. Jeez, he was long and thick and I was full. His hips were wide so my legs were stretching open to accommodate his girth. Nerve endings were being exposed for the very first time and they were happy. The long day, the alcohol, and a wonderful orgasm all came together to render me helpless. I slumped over on him trying to recover. I couldn't. My current state of being didn't faze him. He kept fucking me this way, that way, all damned night. I couldn't even complain. I got myself into this mess. I've just gotta ride it out besides he was my prey, right?

Well, his focused changed, he was now interested in going down on me again. Is that the sun coming up? Damn. I dozed off while he was going down on me. Power nap. I awoke to his asking a question, "Do you have any KY Jelly?" I looked blankly at the ceiling, part of me thinking what the fuck and the other part trying to remember where exactly did I put that KY Jelly? I moved to get up to look for it. He said, "Just tell me, I'll get it." I told him where I thought it was. He came back with it. Torrance got back on the bed; he put the KY Jelly on his finger and started massaging my ass cheeks and rubbing the rim of my anus. I thought, "there is no way that he is gonna put this big ass dick in my ass." Hilarious! He didn't even try; However, he did manage to bring my whole body to life with whatever he was doing just inside my asshole. He continued to fuck me. I came again. He came again.

Finally, about 10 am, he was ready to leave. I was exhausted. I only walked him to the door so I could lock it. When he was leaving, I said "goodbye." He turned, looked at me and said, "I fuck." I thought I misunderstood him. I looked at him with confusion and squinted my eyes like "huh?" He said, "Last night you asked me if I don't talk, drink or dance, what do I do?" I smiled. He said, "Yeah, I fuck that's what I do." He turned and walked away. I shook my head, closed the door and leaned up against it. "Touché Torrance."

Graciousness

very polite in a way that shows respect

Today is the day, finally some long awaited girlfriend time! One of my childhood friends and I have planned to take a drive to a quaint city in North Georgia. The plan is to attend their annual festival, drink, talk, and, hopefully, flirt with the locals while catching up on everything and everybody. Yes, it's going to be fun. We even rented a room at the local motel. We will head home tomorrow after check-out.

Well, as planning goes things happen, changes happen, and revisions happen. About a week before we leave, she and I are chatting it up about our little escape from reality... you know shit like, do we need an armband? How far are the events from the motel? Can we walk? Right, we are hashing out the logistics. Well, she mentions that she's been seeing this guy. She tells me all about him. I'm like, wow he sounds fun and you sound like YOU like him. Afterwards, she goes on to ask about this guy that I've been seeing. I actually met him through her a couple of years before at a local gaming pub. His name was Melvin.

I told her, laughingly, "He's wonderful. I lloooovvveee him." That makes me laugh because I always enjoy that feeling of giddiness when it manages to find me. She laughed because she knows me well. Casually, she said something like "Do you think he would like to come with us for the night?" I answered quickly, "I don't know but I'll ask." Of course, I laid out the plans prior to my asking him. He said, "Sure, I'll ride my bike up." Just like that, our girlfriend weekend changed into a couple's getaway.

Ok, I'm headed to her house. She has volunteered to drive. I'll park my car at her house for the night. When I get there, hugs, laughter, squeals, we are ready to go. First, order of business, I fixed a cocktail because I'm the passenger. Then I loaded my bags and rations into her trunk. She's on the driver side. I'm muthafuckin' NOT! Cheers!

Aye, let's hit it! Once we are moving, she tells me that she has to stop for gas and swing through to pick up her guy. My mind registered her words then I said "ok." No worries, right? Besides, Melvin is coming too. Now, I figured her guy was probably coming but I thought he would meet us there. Whatever, shake those thoughts off, this is gonna be fun. Now, we are gassed up and picking her guy up. We will be on our way in a second. Ok, well maybe a couple of minutes... alright 20 minutes later, too funny! We are off, plot twist, I'm in the backseat now because not only is this man, easy on the eyes, he is tall and big as fuck! Whatever, right? I'm STILL not in the driver's seat. Hilarious.

It took us about an hour and 20 minutes to get there. We stopped a couple of times for randomness. We checked into the motel. Two full-sized beds, a chair, a tv with remote, a mini-fridge and a lamp. Yes, this is exactly a motel. I claimed my bed, closest to the door. If I'm sharing a room with someone, I usually choose the bed nearest to the exit. I have no idea why... self-preservation, I guess. After putting our items away, we took a couple of shots and made drinks to go. It's time to head on over to the festival area. We walked for several minutes, random conversation and laughter filled the air. We looked like friends ready for some fun. As soon as we could see the festival check-in and information booth, we all turn at the sound of a motorcycle. Honestly, I was just trying to move my non-hearing ass out of the way. But when I turned around, I noticed the bike slowing, as it got closer I could see his eyes smiling at me.

Melvin! I took a deep breath. I like this man. He works in IT, computer engineering. Deepest darkest chocolate skin ever, beautiful smile, adventurous and...married. Ughhh... During the time that I was seeing him, I was relationship focused, so I didn't know how to separate his actions from the idea of being in a relationship... ugh whatever!

He comes to a complete stop. I can't even see his mouth but his eyes are smiling bright. I returned the smile gleefully. He never took his eyes off me when he said hello to my friend and her guy. She asked, "Did you get a new bike?" His eyes darted towards the sound of the question. He answered, "Nah, I painted it." They went on talking about the arduous task of taking it apart and blah, blah, blah... He finally looked back at me, "get on" a directive, nothing questionable about it. Before I had a chance to respond, he said to them "We will catch-up with y'all in a few." He helped me up on the bike; I snuggled in, waved good-bye and held on tight. We were only about a mile from the motel; remember before Melvin arrived, the three of us had only been walking for a little while.

At the motel, Melvin assisted with my getting off his bike. He knows that I don't have any biking experience, so he treats me like a newbie. Actually, he knows that I'm pretty inexperienced in many areas. He's always testing my boundaries. We enter the room together. He has to take off his riding attire. I refreshed my drink, sat on the chair and watched. I don't know if we talked at all during this time. I do know that as I watched him, I thought "He is very detailed and patient about removing this gear." He never unsnapped with a rip or tear. He unsnapped each snap one at a time. I could hear the zip unzip one track at a time. He folded each piece, rolled something into a log, hung up his jacket and placed his boots in the closet. Oh, there's a closet? Hmph. I heard him talking. I refocused and viola' he was in front of me... jeans, t-shirt, socks no shoes and a non-descript look upon his face. His energy demanded my attention... I said, "Yes, what did you say? You ready?" I started to stand. He said, "Take your pants off, I want to lick your pussy. That's all I've been thinking about." I looked at him and laughed "stop it." But I noticed this look in his eyes, he was serious. Well damn. I guess the others will wait. I maintained the gaze of his eyes as I reached down to unbutton and unzip my pants, as I'm doing so, I managed to remove my sneakers,

44

using the opposite foot as a tool. Next, I took off my jeans. When I bent over to remove them from legs, Melvin said, "You aren't wearing any panties." I couldn't discern if it was a question or not. It didn't require a response; I wasn't wearing any panties.

Shoes off, socks on, pants off, Melvin walked up to me and kissed me. He was a fucking awesome kisser. His kisses make you blush afterwards because even though you only kissed you feel like you did just a little bit too much with your mouth. I kissed him back. I could feel my caramel center heating up. Yes. He reached down between my legs, just to feel around I guess, his fingers weren't new to that area. I parted my legs, instinctively. He raised his finger and licked it then inserted the same finger into my mouth. It must have tasted yummy to him because he walked forward forcing me to move with him, he asked in the process, "which bed?" I replied "by the door." That's where we went for him to lay me down. He stopped walking me when we reached the foot of the bed. No words, I sat on the bed, scooted up, laid back and spread my legs. He looked, he always looks. I'm blushing because he always referred to it as "beautiful." He's in no hurry and neither am I, not anymore anyway.

Melvin leans down to start his process of licking my pussy. I relax into the bed. He leans down, inhales and exhales his breath onto my clitoris then I feel a soft kiss. He always begins with a kiss. A simple, sweet kiss, kind of like "I've missed you" or "hello." I know that this isn't just a pussy licking moment; he enjoys it way too much. I relax in to this pampering session. Melvin begins his licks, nibbles and tastes. He licks some more. I'm enjoying it. After a couple of minutes, he stops. I open one eye, like what happened? He looks at me and says, "Ok, time to go, you ready?" I laughed "Seriously?" He said, "Yeah, I'll finish later." He continued, "I just know that I wouldn't have been able to enjoy the day without getting that off my mind." I said "Oh ok, give me a second, let me put on my clothes." I went to my suitcase to get panties. He said "no panties." My response while laughing "I'm wet as fuck, I need panties." He just repeated his statement "no panties." Well, fuck, at least, I need to pat some of this dry. So, I headed to the bathroom to calm and dry the juicy beast. Then I finished getting dressed, one last kiss and a strong hug. As he held me, I could feel his hardness pressing up against my leg, damn. We headed out to meet the others.

I walked the same mile as before and while we walked it together, I was filling Melvin in on all the things the three of us talked about during the car ride. He laughed and commented. He told me how much he enjoyed the ride here on his motorcycle. He talked about how beautiful the trees were and how free he felt riding the winding roads. Overall, it was a quick walk. While we walked, I sent a text to check the location of the others. We would be there soon.

We found the pub. We are here! Yay, there was a live band, good people and beer. I'm in heaven. We ordered some food, danced a little, and sampled some beers. We didn't spend much time at any particular place because there were many venues and vendors along this three-mile stretch. As day turned into night, we walked, watched the night fall, drank, everything was love. Melvin is always aware of my presence. He reaches for my hands when I'm done looking or shopping. He anticipates my steps. Damn, I enjoy him. At some point I noticed that the others were gone, I'm not sure if we separated from them or if they separated from us. Either way, we are all grown-ups. Besides we would see them later at the motel anyway, we are sharing a room.

So, Melvin and I sip, look and shop a little more. I'm not sure what time we headed back to the motel. I was lost in time. I'm starting to think that's a gift... the ability to lose time. How awesome would that be? As we were walking back to the hotel, holding hands, not really

46

saying much, I noticed Melvin looking at something to the left of us. Out of curiosity, I looked too. He said, "That's a putt-putt golf course." I just said, "Oh there are some pretty cool designs in there, huh?" I continued with "Maybe you can go there sometime when they are open." He said, "Let's check it out." My internal alarm went off, "Now?" was my response. He laughed and said, "Come on scaredy cat." He was right; I am a rule-follower. He pulled my arm I followed reluctantly. I was looking around. I'm not trying to go to jail in Mayberry tonight.

We walked through the closed putt-putt golf course. We are looking at windmills and streams and the randomness of it all. Finally, I'm relieved, we are leaving. Well, we get to what we thought would be an exit, it wasn't. It was a freaking fence! This n-word looked at me talking about, "I'll help you over." I was like "I'm not going over that damned fence. How do you propose to help me over a 6ft fence?" I was laughing and said, "I'll meet you on the other side. I'm going back the way we came." Well he was not moving, surveying the fence, looking for an exit. I waved good-bye and started on my journey. At some point, I decided that I would find a bench to wait for him. He would be coming this way soon. I noticed how beautiful and clear the night skies were. In this moment of appreciation, I smiled. Oohhh there's a gazebo! I'll wait there. The gazebo resembled a centerpiece on a table of crowded half-eaten plates and glasses. It was beautiful and regal in the midst of this chaotic putt-putt golf disaster. I continued towards the gazebo and sat. My vantage point allowed me to keep an eye out for Melvin and continue star gazing. I had only been sitting for a few moments when he walked up. I smiled at him, he started to chuckle. He said, "I couldn't get out." I shook my head "no, duh!" He entered the gazebo and sat next to me. We talked for maybe 20 minutes.

His energy changed. I sat quietly. I wasn't sure if he were about to say something or just having a personal moment. He placed my hand on his crotch; I felt the electricity shoot up my arm. I looked at him. He wasn't with me anymore. In his mind, he was already getting his dick sucked. I looked around, took a deep breath and changed my body position. I was playing the scenario in my mind. I could get on my knees; no one would see me only a man sitting on a bench, right? So, that's what I did. I moved to the floor of the gazebo. Melvin revealed his dick. Beautiful, hard, thick... the sight of it made me completely forget my concerns about going to jail this evening. I felt safe with him. As any awesome woman would do, I proceeded to suck his dick, outside in a gazebo, in the middle of a putt-putt golf course somewhere in the mountains. I can remember thinking damn it sounds loud here but it was the stillness of the night and sucking, slurping sounds that seemed to magnify in my ears. I had a random thought as I was trying to manufacture more saliva, are there any crickets or frogs around this area? Why is it so fucking quiet? Focus Joy, focus.

Melvin's next words were "sit on it." My reply was an instant "no." He said, "Come on Baby, ain't nobody gonna see us." I was wet as hell, so turned on, seriously, I could use an orgasm. I was adamant "no." Well, after a convincing argument on his part and with the way my body responds to his, I stood up and pulled my jeans down. Lord have mercy, where is my good judgment? Once my pants were down around my knees, I turn my back to Melvin. Picture this, he has one leg out of his pants, with his legs opened, I back into him with my legs together, with the sole intention of sitting down on his dick. Melvin is using his hands to spread my ass and lips open from the back to aid the entry of his dick. Well, it sounds great, right? We had some logistical issues. He has a thick dick and I have a large ass. So, I believe my ass was too big. For whatever reason I couldn't 'just' sit on it. I mentioned earlier that he's an engineer. So, this n-word starts trying figure out the best way for me to bend to allow entry from his sitting position. After a couple of crazy attempts, I end up or rather down, in a downward facing dog position, in this damn gazebo. My feet are together, knees close to my chest, my back arched and my hands are on the ground. Hell, this wasn't even downward facing dog. Whatever it was, finally, he's inside I'm trying to enjoy the moment and hold myself up at the same damn time. I tell him, it's uncomfortable, spread my lips, he did. Now that's better. Finally, we get a little rhythm going. My vision changed suddenly, my brain was trying to register the changes. Melvin says "don't move." At the same time, I realized the change was blue lights. My brain said "Police!" I popped up like a fucking jack in the box. He grabbed and, literally, pushed me down in the floor of the gazebo. I can laugh now but I was scared as hell. As I was sitting on the floor with my bare ass on the ground, I kept thinking, how was I going to tell my Mom for what I was arrested? In addition, I hope nothing crawls on my cooch! Yes, those were my true thoughts at 40 something. For the next several minutes, we were silent. The lights went away, eventually.

Melvin had the nerve to say "ok come on." I stood up and started pulling up my pants. He was like "What are you doing? Sit back on it." I looked at him and serious as hell said, "Fuck this. I'm leaving." He started laughing. Telling me they weren't coming for us blah, blah, blah... I dressed. He dressed. We started retracing our steps to the motel. My heart was racing. I was so nervous.

When we got back to hotel, the other couple was there. They were in the shower. Melvin and I made drinks and turned one some music. I can't remember anything significant happening. We were just four adults in a motel room on a mini excursion. The other couple got out of the shower then onto the bed messing around. I winked at them and headed to wash my, literal, ass because of the fear of the creepy crawlies from the gazebo floor. After my shower, I entered the room,

Melvin was telling them about our close call with the Police. They were laughing. I was not amused. By now, I'm so annoyed that I was going to bed.

I laid down. Everyone continued to talk around me; which was fine because I didn't want to talk. I was unhappy, scared, having an internal temper tantrum. My friend and Melvin both recognized my current state of being. Well, she turned her attention to her guy. Melvin turned his attention me. I was pretending to be asleep. Melvin leans over and whispers in my ear, "I'm giving you some time to get it together, but the next song that comes on I want you to dance for me...naked." My eyes popped open. I was thinking "I ain't doing shit." He registered my alarm and anger. Before I could say anything aloud, he said, "I'm using a 'yes'." I took a deep breath and closed my eyes tighter.

Ok, some background, a few months ago, I started giving him an extra "yes'" to use whenever he wanted. Like a bonus, it's actually kind of fun. For example, if he did something that I thoroughly enjoyed, I would give a "yes" he could use it whenever he wanted. Well, tonight he has chosen to-muthafuckin-night to redeem a "yes." Ugh now I have to dance in front of these people and Melvin...naked.

My next words, "I need a drink" and "let me get my shoes." I can't remember the song that was playing but it was ending soon. However, I will remember the next song forever. Well, I'm upright trying to play fair; I mean seriously, it's my game. I can't renege can I? I swallowed my drink in one gulp. I poured another. Put on my heels. The song is ending. I remember thinking, "I don't know how to dance naked. Ugghhh! This man...damn!

Song ends. I'm ready. Maybe it's something fast and upbeat but it wasn't. "Ciara's *Body Party.*" Oh, my goodness, this song is sexy as hell, which reminded me that "I'm sexy as hell." So, I started moving from side to side. I was trying to get a groove going in my head. Melvin was sitting on the side of the bed watching me. I had to keep my eyes closed or look away. I've always struggled with the idea of people watching me. Like what are they thinking? I know I was bashful a couple of times, one being when I removed my t-shirt. I don't know what I was expecting to happen but he kept watching. I completed a few turns. Then I danced with my back facing him, shaking my ass a couple of times, I laughed, as I felt the fear and anger lift. The song seems to have played forever.

Melvin hugged me and told me that I had done a great job. He said, "You are a great dancer." I rolled my eyes and was like "whatever. How many yes' do you have left? You better be glad that I love you." He said "If you don't know, I'm not telling you. I love you too." I felt better. Now, it was our time to get into bed for some playtime. Under the covers, we touched and kissed and bit secret places. Passion. Love. We listened to the love made by our roommates. I wanted to watch. He said "Watch, they don't care." I couldn't bring myself to peek.

I felt even more aroused listening to their sounds. I reached deeper into the cover to find Melvin's hardness. Well, my hand was grasping where it was supposed to be. Though, he was flaccid. I find his face. I ask, "Are you not having a good time?" He said "I'm having a wonderful time." Ok, so I took it upon myself, to try to help us reach an erection. I proceeded to give him a blow-job. Nothing. He doesn't seem to be phased by this period of inaction. So, I figure this isn't the first time that he's experienced this; However, I'm taking it personally. As I'm sucking his dick, I start reflecting on the erections we wasted throughout the day. My mind is literally taking responsibility for something that has nothing to do with me. Like, I should've insisted that we made love when he first got here and, not to mention, I should've been more open to completing our exploits at the gazebo. I'm stressing the fuck out while he's chilling. Well if he's unbothered I think we should switch positions. Hell, I'd love to cum all over his face and beard. At this point, I'm ready to come all over my own hand.

So, I stop sucking, crawl up his body, until I was straddling his face. He wasn't given a choice as he watched me. He didn't say a thing. He just pulled the comforter up to cover his body. So, here I am, thighs wide, hands braced on the wall, waiting for him to stick his tongue in to start this ride. He obliged. I allowed him enough room to breathe. It may have been too much space between us because soon after he started he reached up and grabbed my thighs to pull me closer. I was in a perfect position on my knees to allow my hips to rock back and forth rhythmically. I was feeling that shit. My nipples were rock hard. The area above my clitoris was rubbing the space between his mouth and his nose. I was fucking his face. I could feel my body about to explode. I ground harder; I wanted his whole face inside of me. I said aloud, "I'm cumming." Of course, he couldn't talk but he held me tighter, letting me know that he was ready. Spasms shook my body; I came without regard to our guests or neighbors or the police. As a matter of fact, "Fuck the police!" Hilarious. I'm just teasing. I love the police.

So, I rolled into the bed next to Melvin and fell asleep. I knew that at some point in the night or early morning he would wake me to release his desires once they awakened. Sleep took over where the beer, booze and fear left off. I remember waking up to the sound of rain falling and the feel of Melvin's hard penis pressing against my ass. I rolled over on my back; he moved on top of me and made love to me in the quiet hours of the room we shared with two others. Damn, I liked him.

52

Optimism:

expecting good things to happen

Toby and I met through a dating app, let's call it Firestarter. I'm not sure of the exact month but I do recall that it was chilly enough for a sweater and boots. Not to mention, we met in the Southern part of the US, east of the Mississippi.

We texted and talked for a day then decided to meet for dinner on the following day. He seemed interesting from our conversations. I mean he said he graduated from an HBCU (Historically Black Colleges and Universities), for the life of me I can't remember which; and he's been an educator for over 20 years.

We met in the parking lot of a restaurant that was about 20 miles or so from where I was staying. We stood there and chatted for a bit. He was a country boy with country boy charm, tall, solid, beautiful smile, good-looking enough... Now, you know those were my private thoughts, as well as, hmm yeah, he could get it! I have a tendency to be pretty outspoken. So, I said aloud, "Toby, why don't you follow me back to my hotel? We can grab a bite near there." He didn't hesitate. We got into our respective automobiles. He led. I followed. Besides he was more familiar with the area than me.

Let me back up for a second, when I got to the restaurant, he was already there. He was standing beside a big truck, something like a Dodge Ram, waving at me as I pulled into the parking lot. For whatever reason, I thought that was his truck. However, when he left to get his car, he returned in a Honda Accord hatchback, maybe a 1998 or 1999. I kept thinking like "Why is he driving that car in 2015?" But I resigned to the idea that maybe it was his tinker toy; especially, since it had a college fraternity on the front tag. So, no worries, I followed Toby listening to music and trying, desperately, to minimize my thoughts.

When we pulled up to the hotel, he parked and got out with a duffle bag. I laughed to myself thinking, that was presumptuous. I pulled up behind him, stopped and said "Get in the car with me, I'll drive to dinner and I need to make a couple of stops." He was like cool, walked to my car, put his bag in the back seat and got into the front. Once settled inside, I asked, "What's up with the bag?" He laughed and said, "Oh I went to my daughter's for the weekend, so it was just in the car." I nodded my head, in understanding. We pulled off.

Me: "Do you want to go to dinner before I run my errands?"

Him: "It doesn't matter, whatever you want."

Me: "Alright. I need to grab some Vodka and stop in the pharmacy. We can hit those first."

Off we go, using the GPS, I locate the package store which I have visited before. He tells me as we are getting out, how much he loves vodka. We have a regular conversation about our favorite brands of vodka. As we are entering the store, he reaches for my hand and holds it. Strange, right? Well, I thought so, but anyway I went with it. So, we get inside. We are walking around the store hand-in-hand, he points out the vodka he likes but he doesn't pick it up... hmm, side eye, what? I just said, "Oh yeah, I've tried that before". Then proceeded to pick up a liter of my favorite gluten-free vodka. He frowned and was like "Bae, I haven't had that before." I just laughed and said "You'll be fine, it's vodka." Now, what's funny about this is that whether he was with me or not, I was planning to buy vodka. So, no worries.

We walk to the counter hand in hand. Well before the clerk could ring up the purchase, Toby dropped my hand, and he did this spin off move towards the front of the store. It was so weird. The clerk and

I looked at each other to acknowledge the awkwardness of the moment. Anyway, he totaled my purchase, I swiped my card, and the bottle was placed in the bag along with the receipt. Well, now Toby comes back to collect the bag and take my hand as we walked out of the store. I giggled on the inside, thinking what the fuck? But I can't really say anything because I don't know him. You know? Maybe this is what he knows... He opened the driver-side door for me, placed the package on the backseat, and then got into the car. Now, we are both buckled in, chatting about random topics as we head to the drug store. My list was pretty short; three specific items, a new nail polish, facial cleanser wipes and panty liners.

Well, we enter the store, hand in hand. Yeah, it's odd to me but I'll live through it. The cosmetics section is on the wall immediately to the right upon entrance, I stop to look at nail polishes.

Him: "What are you looking for?"

Me: "I have to polish my toes. I need new polish."

Him: "Can I polish your toes? I want to choose the color?"

Me: (with a big smile) "Yes, please, I'd like that."

So, he stayed there looking to make a choice from a myriad of colors. I strolled off to collect my other two items.

Toby finds me in the store. He walks up behind me, wraps his big strong arms around me, as I snuggled into his hug. I mean why not? If we are pretending to be in love, holding hands and shit, let me at least enjoy the hugs. He held up his nail polish choice, I acknowledged with a "yyyeesss, I love that color" and took it from his hand. He then leans down and whispers in my ear... "I don't have any condoms." Of course, I laughed, because I can be silly and an airhead. I turned to look at him and replied, "We are in a drug store crazy, go get some." He left in search of condoms. I headed to the front of the store with three items in hand. After a few minutes, Toby joined me in the front, I saw him stop to pick up some Cranberry juice along the way. Now, we are in line, I have my three items and he has his two items. I looked at the brand of condoms in his hands, Magnum XL 12 pack. Instantly, I felt warm all over. Reader? Stay focused, I know I can be shallow and petty at times. No judgment...

Now it's my turn to check out, I placed my three items on the counter. Well, low and behold, guess who places their items on the counter with mine and then twirls the fuck off? Toby! Is this n-word a ballerina or something? But instead it dawns on me, he doesn't have any money. Ugh Joy what have you gotten yourself into? So, I smile at the cashier and pay for the items. I'm laughing as I think about that night. Being the southern gentleman that he was, he came back to carry the bags. As if we have established a routine, he opened my door and closed it after I'm inside, placed the packages on the back seat and then he got in.

Leaving the parking lot, we start talking about dinner options.

Him: "Do you like steak?"

Me: "Yes, I do. What do you have in mind?"

Him: "There's a great steak house down the street, it's called Morton's."

Me: "Yep, I know, I had lunch there yesterday."

Him: "Do you want steak?"

Me: "Not necessarily but they have a great veggie plate. I can order that."

Him: "Well, if you aren't gonna have steak, let's go someplace else."

Me: "Oohh look a Wendy's!"

Him: "Ok, that's great. We can have steak tomorrow."

I was driving and thinking a hundred thoughts, "Tomorrow, ain't no tomorrow." "Doesn't he have to work tomorrow?" Lastly, "I'm not buying this grown ass man a steak dinner!" He can order a value meal large w/cheese. That's all I'm paying for, for his broke ass! We are in the car driving, he's holding my hand, talking and we laugh together, at something on the radio. I'm telling my brain to slow down. Damn, I need a drink.

The drive-thru window has a long line of cars. So, we parked to go inside to place our order. He jumped out of the car, a little extra spring in his step. Maybe he was hungry. He came around to open my door, and he took my hand to assist me as I stepped out. Yep, we entered Wendy's hand in hand. There's a line, so, we stood there waiting for several minutes before placing our orders. He allowed me to order first, "junior bacon cheeseburger, value fry". After I ordered, I sat on a bench in the waiting area. He ordered next. I listened closely. "Double all the way with cheese add bacon value meal with a Coke, large." I smiled a wicked smile because I already knew. Well, get this shit, he completes his order and twirls over to talk to the grill master about making his burger fresh. He told him that he wants to watch him make his burger to make sure that he doesn't mess up. I'm like "We are in fucking Wendy's," they know how to make your trifling ass burger! Out of the corner of my eye, I notice the cashier standing there looking at him and then at me. I mouth to her "did he pay?" She shook her head no. So, I got up to pay. I return to my seat, legs crossed waiting patiently trying to figure out if I was seriously this desperate for companionship.

After our order was complete, Toby carried our bags out of the store. Y'all know the rest... So, now we are headed back to my hotel.

When we get to the hotel, I parked by the back entrance. I wasn't the least bit interested in having the guest services or concierge see me enter with this guest. Toby got out of the car, came around to open my door, he also opened the passenger door behind me and then walked back around to his side of the car. I stopped looked and thought, "Did this m-effer just open the door so I could get the bags out?" I started laughing. He looked at me and said "what's funny?" I shook my head, took a deep breath and reached inside for the bags closest to me. Of course, he got his duffle bag and the food.

We entered the hotel; I scanned the surrounding areas, just checking to see who I can see and, honestly, hell, who sees me...with him. At the elevator, I press the up button. Toby commented that he was at this hotel before for a conference. That was our conversation on the way up. Exiting the elevator, we took a left, 806. Keyless entry, door opened.

Reader, if you don't know this about me now, you will by the end of this book. I am big on presentation. I take my time. I like for as much as possible to be as close to great, as possible. Every occasion is an event, even when I'm alone. I love enjoying myself. In this case, that means, I've gotta turn on some music, pour myself a drink, unpack my packages, food last. By that time, I'll be ready to sit down to eat. Well, tonight is no different, other than the fact that I have a guest.

So, cue the music, iPad on Pandora. I said to Toby, "I'll be right back." I was going down the hall to get ice. I left. I believe I was gone for about 2 minutes. I returned to the room, humming to the tune streaming down the hall. Getting groovy in my head because that's what I do. I walk into the room, asking at the same time, would you like for me to make you a drink now? I stopped dead in my tracks. I was stunned at the site of this grown ass man shoving his burger in his mouth like it was his first meal in a long ass time. After I realized that I was staring, I forced myself to continue doing my own thing. In my head though, I was laughing hard as fuck, like this can't be happening. So, while I was fixing my drink, this thought crossed my mind, "He better be glad he has a big dick." With that thoughtful nugget tucked away, I continued. So, now I have my music playing, drink made, nail polish and remover on the table, condoms on the night stand, now I can prepare to have dinner.

Secretly, hoping that he hasn't eaten my food too. I walk over to where Toby is sitting, to get the bag which should contain my burger and fries. Though, I notice, while in stride, that there is a burger and fries lying on the desk. Wait! Huh? Where's the bag? Would you believe this... joker, ugh I've gotta stop using n-word, has torn the bag open and is using it as a napkin to wipe his hands and mouth. Now, I can't even laugh anymore. I was like "Oh my freaking goodness." I gathered my wits and asked, "Toby, would you like a napkin or wet cloth?" He said, "Nah, I'm good." I simply replied "ok." Now in this moment, I twirled to retrieve my dinner from the desk. I went to take a seat in the sitting area. Now I have my food, my drink and the music is playing. Yes, I'm having an awesome time. Life is good. Grace. I am grateful for a yummy meal and the ability not to sweat the small stuff.

As I was about to take the first bite of my burger, Toby came over and sat beside me. We started talking, cool. Finally, I bit my burger.

He reached for my foot, trying to take my boot off and talking about how sexy I am. Well, thank you, I appreciate your kind words. Let me help you with that... You know what that means? Down, to the table NOT my throat, goes my burger. I stopped eating to remove my boots and socks. He seems to be pretty anxious about getting started on painting my toes. Oh well, I can eat while he removes the old and polishes with the new, right? Wrong. He announced that he didn't want to remove the old polish, if I could do that, please? Of course, not a problem at all; besides, I would've done that anyway. Burger and fries are waiting patiently on the table. As I removed the polish, randomness filled the air along with the music and smells of polish remover. One foot complete, inhale. Let me make a drink. I think I'll have a double right now, exhale, and then take one to my comfy spot on the sofa. Chick this shit is crazy.

Now, all ten toes have been removed of polish, rinsed, and prepared for Toby to apply his fabulous hot pink nail polish that he chose and I paid for. Ugghh that wasn't nice, I shouldn't have said that. Oh well, I returned to the sofa, picked up my dinner and propped my feet up on the table, I'm ready, he's ready. He asked excitedly "Are you ready?" I replied with the same level of enthusiasm "Yes, go for it." He sat on the table by my feet. He began to paint my toes. He told the story about his knee injury from college. Which is why he can't kneel on the floor. I tried to eat my burger... cold. He continued his story by saying that if he wasn't injured he would've gone pro. Fries...colder. He feels bad because he let a lot of people down. He wanted to take care of his momma. We started asking each other a question at the same time. I laughed and said, "You go first." He said, "Look, do you like your toes? I did a good job, didn't I? I love this color. What do you think?" Before I realized what was coming out of my mouth, I said "You did an awesome job! Yay, you. You should be proud of yourself." Can you believe I said that to a grown ass man? I felt like I was talking to a child. Bless his heart. I really looked at him

61

observing the lines in his face, the gray in his beard and mustache, the glint in his eyes. Then, I asked my question, "How old are you again?" He smiled big and bright ".52." Big exhalation. In my mind, I thought, "jeez I hope his big hungry, country, proud of his artwork ass can fuck."

As if reading my mind, which I doubt, Toby was ready for action. He told me "Girl, you make me crazy, I can't wait any longer, I've gotta have you right now." Now, remember I told y'all with me timing is everything. I'm like wait, my toes, sad face, I'm hungry, I want to shower, sad face, now I'm unhappy. Hilarious. He's tearing at my clothes telling me all the stuff he's gonna do to me. I will myself to get with the moment. Be spontaneous everyone says. I tell my inner temper-tantrum to chill the fuck out. Let's get this dick.

So, now I'm naked lying on the bed. He's getting naked while at the same time opening a condom. This m-effer is off to the races. I'm like is it time for the condom already. He's not going to go down on me? I didn't shower so let me do a quick taste test. Well, it tastes good to me but hell I'm biased. How the fuck would he know, he hasn't been close enough to it to smell or taste it? Well, hold on, cause here he comes in all his naked glory! I'm lying back on my elbows attempting to watch the show. He hurriedly comes to the bed, condom on. I'm trying to anticipate his movement. Well, he puts a knee on the bed between my legs and with his upper body pushes me back and proceeds to put his dick inside of me. I'm dying laughing. Seriously, in all my years of being sexually active, I've never seen anything like it. So, he's in, it's a nice size, I'm like ok cool, I'll ride this out. Well, in, out, in, out, in, out, in and shudder. This n-word has shot his load. Breathing hard, talking about, he shouldn't have eaten such a big meal beforehand, that I was just too sexy and what a long day he has had. I was lying under him trying desperately not to laugh out loud or show any signs of disappointment. I applied pressure to his shoulder to get him to roll off of me. Before I left for the shower he said two more things: "I'm sorry Bae, I'm gonna make it up to you", and, "You aren't gonna eat this, are you?", referring to my burger and fries. I said, "Nope, you can have it." I grabbed my drink, pivoted on my heels, hurried to the bathroom, turned on the shower, and grabbed a towel to put over my mouth while I laughed myself to tears.

Shower over, laughing done, tears dried. I'm cool, calm and collected, once again. I enter the room to find Toby, just as I hoped, asleep. I went to the other bed, turned the sheets and comforter back. Grabbed my iPad, and switched from music to current book. This is what my alone time feels like. There wasn't a need to wake Toby, he seems like he needs the rest and I don't really want to be bothered. Eventually, I went to sleep. At some point during the early morning hours, I was awakened by movement in the room. It took me a moment to collect myself, why is someone in here with me then I remembered...Toby. First, thought, I hope this nigga ain't trying to come over here with me. I sat up turned on a lamp but I didn't see him. I realized that he was in the bathroom. I took this time to scan for my personal belongings, remembering that I had placed the valuables in a drawer.

He came out of the bathroom. He looked refreshed. I guess he was well rested and showered. I notice he's carrying his duffle bag. I glanced around the room once more. Then I ask, "Where did you put the rest of the condoms?" He replied, "Oh they are in my bag, I thought you wouldn't need them." I thought really? But instead I said "Why don't we split the pack? You keep six." He said "ok" then took them out and left me five on the chest. He said, "I'm leaving now." From the bed, I said, "Ok cool. It was nice meeting you. Take care." His last question was "What time do they start serving breakfast?" "Is it free?" I replied "I don't know." Toby left. I went back to sleep.

When I awoke, I put on my music, got dressed for the gym and started picking up around the room. Before, I left the room, I had a thought, housekeeping will come before I get back. So, I attempted to put all the towels in the floor in the bathroom but... WAIT! Where are the fucking towels? Did this m-effer steal the towels? Oh Lord. I sent Toby a text.

Me: "Did you take the towels out of the bathroom?"

Toby: "Yes, they were dirty."

Me: "What? The hotel washes their own towels!"

Me: "Never mind. Did you take my bra?"

Toby: "What color was it?"

Fuck it. I'm done. No more. These thoughts were followed by uncontrollable laughter and an awesome workout in the gym. I completed my stay expecting two additional charges to my room: breakfast and three sets of towels.

Detachment:

lack of emotion or personal interest

This is what I remember about this particular Sunday afternoon. I am standing in the airport waiting on my flight to nowhere in particular. I love taking these mini excursions. Seriously, I was flying into New York, definitely one of my favorite cities. I had not made any plans beyond my flight. I mean its NYC everything is possible. Here I am... waiting. I was wearing a deep green sundress with black stripes, no bra. I was comfortable in about a 2in wedge. I was talking on the phone, I can't remember to whom, but I was leaning up against a makeshift temporary construction wall...talking, laughing and waiting. I never pay attention to anyone at the airport but on this day, I noticed a woman carrying a mesh bag of clothing. I kinda frowned and thought, "Eh I hope those aren't dirty clothes." I erased the thought, why the fuck do I care?

Finally, it's time to board, my seat is at the back of the plane, possibly because I booked last minute. There are four seats in this row on the left side of the aisle. As of this moment, there are three of us seated. The seat to my immediate right was empty. The last passenger had boarded and the cabin doors are secure blah, blah, blah announcement blared from overhead. With that, I figured at this point, the seat to my right would remain empty... Lucky me! Well, I celebrated just a tad bit early because as I was looking down at my hands in my laps thinking about nothing and waiting for take-off, when my eyes focused upward to search for the deep, rich voice, which said "Excuse me." I looked up and up some more. I didn't respond immediately because my brain wasn't comprehending how this man filled this whole space and, not to mention, how was he going to fit in this seat? Finally, I spoke, "oh I'm sorry. I began to move into the aisle with the passenger to my left to allow this giant man to pass and to watch him squeeze into this seat. Well, after a minute or so, everyone has settled and we are preparing for take-off. Because my new neighbor's shoulders were wide, I found myself sitting against the seat behind his shoulder. That seemed to be a more comfortable position for me than sitting up. He was friendly. I am friendly. We started talking immediately. He has an accent, nothing that I recognized but I'm listening for common sounds and inflections to ensure I respond appropriately.

Well, as it turns out, he's Ghanaian. He told me that he was from Ghana. Just to be clear I asked "Ghana" or "Guyana." He clarified Ghana, located in West Africa. Ok, I got it. He lives and works as a police officer in New York City. His size probably comes in handy with that job. He and his woman friend have been on vacation in the Caribbean somewhere. I asked, "Where is she?" He pointed absently towards the front of the plane. I followed with "Would you like for me to switch seats with her so that you all could sit together?" He shook his head "no." I shrugged "ok," whatever. He went on to tell me about their vacation. He had a great time, snorkeling, sky diving, lots of cocktails. He was smiling as he talked. He has magnificent teeth. His smile reached his eyes when he talked. We talked the whole flight. I noticed his leg pressing against mine when the plane experienced some turbulence. My first analogous thought was "tree trunk." Jeez, am I having a hot flash? I instinctively reached out to grab anything in reach, which happened to be his leg. Whatever, I wanted to touch his leg! It was firm and big as fuck. He did not flinch. Wait now, keep in mind, I'm sitting with my shoulder behind his. So, my lower arm is resting on the arm rest under his, kinda inter-locked. Therefore, my grabbing this man's thigh was purely a reflex action. Too funny!

The plane settled. We kept talking and laughing. He lowered his voice "Will you put my number in your phone?" I said sure, I pulled out my phone and opened 'notes' where I proceeded to enter his name Randy and number. I didn't add it to my directory because I knew that I wasn't going to call him. Save. Swipe. I put my phone away. We continued to talk. He told me that I had a beautiful smile.

67

I thanked him. He went on to say, "While we were waiting for the flight, I was watching you on your phone, laughing and talking. The whole time, I was thinking, I wish I were on the other end of that phone." His look changed. He added "I want to make you laugh, to laugh with you." I really thought that was nice, so I replied, "I'm laughing with you now. We've been laughing since take-off." He smiled at that too. For the first time we had a few minutes of mutual silence. The pilot announced our descent and approximate time before landing. Randy pulled out his phone and handed it to me. I looked at him like "yes?" He said, "Will you put your number in my phone? I want to see you again." I handed it back while at the same time saying, "I already have yours, I'll call you." He looked at me and said, "No you won't." He was right. I reached into my purse, retrieved a business card and handed it to him. This is my business you can reach me here. Fuck it. I'm exhausted with men and text messages. He took it, looked at it and said, "Thank you, I'll call you." I smiled and thought sure you will.

We talk a little more but I'm too excited now. I can see the city. New York has my undivided attention. The plane lands safely. Randy and I say good-bye and both think that it was a pleasure meeting each other. As we are exiting, I'm scanning the plane looking for his travel companion. Curiosity, I guess. Who is the woman that sleeps under this beautiful Ghanaian giant? Lucky her. Randy hugs me after we exit, I try to climb him... just kidding. I hug him back. He joins his companion and walks off. I don't ever see her face but she was the woman with the mesh bag of clothes. Hmm...

I'm in New York bitches! Now, what? As I went to get my luggage, I kept thinking hire a car or take the train? Where am I going? Hmm I decided on a car.

Before I make a move beyond the baggage claim, I sat down for a second to review my notes, what did I want to see and do during this visit? First on the list, visit Brooklyn. Ok, so tonight, I guess I'm staying in Brooklyn. Cool. Whenever, I embark upon these excursions, my plans are loose. My goal is to be in the mix. So, I put myself directly in the mix. I requested a car and headed to this boutique hotel off Flatbush.

Well, it was about 7:00pm, I was sitting on the hotel roof-top having a beer and listening to the sounds of the city. I picked up a six-pack on my way into the hotel but there isn't a fridge, damn boutique. Oh well, I'll drink them all tonight. I'm chilling in my alone time. I've learned to embrace it… that's a whole other story. My phone ringing invaded my revelry, I just swiped "hello." I hear Randy's heavy accent "Joy?" I replied "yes." He says laughing, "I was thinking I would leave a message with your answering service." I laughed, "Nope, I answered." He said, "Are you working?" I said, "Nope. I've just recently checked into my hotel." He follows with, "Where?" I think quickly, "Do I want him to know where I am?" There are literally thousands of hotels in this city. Nonchalantly, I answered, "Brooklyn." Randy said excitedly, "I live in Brooklyn." I thought to myself, do you now? But instead, I said "Oh that's cool."

"I'm sitting here on the roof-top having a beer." He asked hesitantly, "Are you alone?" I laughed and said "duh! You know that I'm alone. Didn't we just talk about this on the plane?" He laughed and agreed. Eventually, he asked, "Can I change your plans for the evening?" Well, it didn't really matter to me because I didn't have any plans per se; and not to mention, I wasn't necessarily interested in anything because I'm taking in the night sounds of Brooklyn. So, without much interest, I said "Go ahead, I'm listening." He proceeded to tell me about this Jamaican restaurant and dance hall. He talked about the good food and cocktails. He said that on Sunday evenings they have a live band and dancing... As he was talking, I was thinking...Hmm a live band and dancing! Randy's silence prompted my attention. I mumbled "huh? What did you say?" He repeated his question "Can I change your plans? What do you say?" I was stuck on live band and dancing. I mean, seriously, what are the chances of me taking in the sites with a Brooklyn local? After careful thought, I responded with my own questions, "Where is this place?" and "Can I meet you there?" For whatever reason, I am not the least bit interested in him coming to my chill spot. He explained that he could pick me up, you know how driving in New York is dangerous and whatever else. I agreed but insisted on meeting him. I'm a big girl, right? Ok now, it's all settled, he's going to send me the address via text message and we would meet at 9:30pm.

With plans in play, I begin my leisurely ritual of getting dressed. After selecting an outfit for dancing, with beer in hand and music playing, I head to the shower. Summertime in New York means I have to let my shoulders breathe, so I chose, from my very limited wardrobe, a paisley halter jumpsuit with comfortable black wedges. Who knows how much I may end up walking in the city? With that thought, at some point during the process of getting ready, I decide that if I like Randy, maybe I'll let him drive me back...

I give myself the once over in the mirror. Aloud I say, "You are looking good Chick!" For whatever reason, I wasn't convinced but oh well. Anyway, it's time to go! I grabbed my cell and purse. While heading to the elevator, I pull up the app to order a car. The car will probably arrive before I do... it is Brooklyn!

I called Randy to let him know that I would be leaving the hotel in three minutes. We confirmed our meeting time and place for 9:30pm. He went on to say that, he would get there a few minutes early to get us a table. Perfect!

70

I'm looking at the arriving car, correct make and model, I look through the window at the driver and say "hi." He says, "Joy?" I responded, "Yes, let me check your tag." I walked around the car to complete my final check to ensure this is the correct driver. Cool. I proceeded to get in the car.

We talked for about 20 minutes as he drove me to the Jamaican spot. That's the best part of ordering a driver, the randomness of the conversation. We pulled up and I hopped out. "Thanks a bunch." "Have a great time", he said. I waved good-bye. He took off.

As I entered the restaurant, I took a deep breath. My energy was off and I could feel it. I felt like I was walking outside of myself. Hmm what was that about? Oh well, I'm here now. I can smell the food, hear the band and feel the excitement in the air. I hope that I can become engrossed in the atmosphere. I stop for a moment, just to become acclimated and to seek out Randy's giant form. Ha! There he is. Our eyes met at the same time. He smiled. I smiled. He got up and proceeded to walk over. While at the same time, I began walking to him. Somewhere in the space between us we met, hugged and he said "It's so good to see that smile again." I relaxed a little. He took my hand, I followed him to our table. It was in a great location within the restaurant. We could see the dance floor and band stand.

Randy insisted on ordering for the table; which was fine with me, because I love for men to order for me. He's a big guy, so we ended up with a few different selections, with my favorite being the curried goat. So, I ate most of that. We drank the traditional Red Stripe beer and sampled a few random cocktails. After dinner, we danced and laughed and hugged and kissed. The longer we danced, the more comfortable we became in each other's space. For the first time during the evening, I felt good but I was still watching myself from a distant place. It was probably midnight or so, when I asked Randy,

"At what time do you work tomorrow?" He replied, "I'm still on vacation until after the 4th." I nodded my head and mumbled "cool." That's all of the information I needed to keep dancing. AYE, no alarm clock for either of us. He was right, the band was amazing. Even during the band breaks, we were still able to dance to some hot tunes. Kudos to Randy! We stayed until about 2am. He asked if I would be taking a car back to my hotel. I said, "I can." He said, "Well, I'd like to make breakfast for you, can I take you back?" I thought for a moment, "Well I'm allergic to eggs but sure you can take me back." He was good with that. I waited inside while he went to retrieve his car.

Once inside of his car, we chatted about randomness. He was telling me of what he knows of the city as he drove. He talked about coming to the United States 15 years ago. The various languages which he spoke fluently. His family in Ghana. I just listened, I didn't feel the need to divulge any information about myself. I wasn't holding back. I just wasn't talking. He talked about American women. He talked about women from the South. He mentioned what good cooks the women from the South were, he then asked, "Will you cook for me while you are here?" I answered plainly without much thought, "no." He laughed and asked "Oh, wow, you don't know how to cook?" I smiled at him puzzled trying to figure out how this conversation suddenly became about me, I laughed softly and continued, "Of course, I can cook; though, I don't feel the need to cook for men from which I don't feel genuineness and love." He laughed a big laugh and said something like "Well, maybe you'll want to cook for me one day." I returned the smile "maybe." We rode in silence for a few moments and he said "Well, until then, I will cook for you." I didn't reply.

Well as soon as we got to Randy's home, he began to prepare breakfast. Interesting... I thought. There was rice and fish, something

72

with ginger and wine. The conversation was nice, his home was warm and welcoming. It was kept by a woman; I sensed that. About 4:30am, he asked, if I wanted to go to sleep, he offered me the couch, but at this time, I had already decided that I wanted to fuck. How could I tell him that? I thought about it a hundred times throughout the night, he was kind, generous and good-looking, why wasn't I feeling anything else? So, I just opened my mouth and the words seemed to float from a different place... "No thank you, I don't want to sleep but I would like to fuck, if you don't mind." He just looked at me. We looked at each other. I was definitely uncomfortable with the words that came out of my mouth. His facial expression reflected my feelings. Instead of replying, Randy stood and went to get something from the kitchen. I sat, not feeling any harm or anything for that matter, just sat, waiting.

Well he returned with two tapered candles in brass candle holders and another bottle of wine. He placed those items on the table and changed the music to something slow. It dawned on me, he was shifting gears to romance. Unfortunately, I wasn't interested. I tried to get my mind to play along but it wouldn't. So, I sat there, waiting and thinking. He poured another glass of wine, I drank it. He sat close, I moved closer. He touched my face, I let him. He twirled his finger in my hair, I touched his face. Ok, so I'm finally able to play along. I reached to refill my wine glass. He noticed and poured. Finally, he leaned in to kiss me. I opened my lips. He was a good kisser, gentle, patient. He's so big, I would've expected more aggression but that wasn't the case.

The music continued, he touched more. I allowed his hands to explore my body. He was moving like a prop engine slowing with the contact of every cloud. Honestly, I wanted him to blow through my skies like a jumbo jet. I had to tell myself to slow down, patience. Instead of enjoying the sensation of this man's hands and lips on me,

73

I was becoming annoyed. I just wanted to feel the weight of his body on mine and explode into oblivion for a few moments. That is all.

Randy proceeds to remove my jumpsuit and panties; he wants to go down on me. Now, we are getting somewhere. Time literally stopped. I'm sure he's doing a great job but his efforts weren't being rewarded by my mind or body. I laid there thinking about all the sights I wanted to see while I explored Brooklyn in a few hours. I feel him moving up. I am thoughtful for a moment; could he tell that I wasn't into it? He presses his lips onto mine. I can feel his dick pressing up against my leg and the heat resonated through my body. Hell, I should've reached out to touch this an hour ago. Now, my body and mind are beginning to communicate. It's about time. I open my lips wider to receive a deeper kiss. I can taste my sweetness on his lips. He squeezed my breast, hips and thighs. I laugh now as I'm thinking about it, he was probably checking to see if I were alive, after my lack of response to him. I tried to spread my legs, to get him closer to the mark. He held me firm with his body and continued to kiss and nibble and explore my breast, neck and face. I'm more responsive now. Thanks to the wine. My mind no longer has to function. My body has taken over. I notice changes in my breathing. Randy's hip movements are simulating that he's already inside of me. When I attempted to open my legs, this time it was allowed. I can now feel his heat laying against my labia. My body is screaming, open me, insert. He reached for a condom. Funny, that small detail never crossed my mind. I took a deep breath and prayed for ecstasy. He laid his head on my chest and lifted his buttocks. I can feel his arms move between us as he put on the condom. He reached his hand between my legs to slide his finger between my lips. The thought that crossed my mind, "Wetness don't fail me now. Please don't reflect my voided mental space." His finger separated my lips and slid as if moving upon silk. I'm thinking, "Yes, thank you, I'm ready."

74

I exhaled deeply. Randy moved above me using his arms as braces. He was looking for something in my eyes and face. He smiled slightly; in return, I swallowed and closed my eyes. There wasn't anything for him there. He leaned down for another kiss. He then used his knees to push my knees open and legs further apart to accommodate the width of his body. As they moved further apart, I could feel the tension of my joints straining to make room for him. Once he stopped, I realized that I was so open under this man, like literally captive under this giant of a Ghanaian. He lowered his whole body at once. Can I support the weight of him? Am I able to sustain the pressure he exudes?

Why haven't I grabbed his dick yet?

Randy doesn't use his hand to aid his entry. He uses his dick as a guide to my entrance. After a few moments it dawns on both of us, his guide needs some assistance. Reluctantly, I reached down to aid his entry. First, I grabbed his hardness, thinking I'd just place the tip of it at the entrance and allow him to move on from there. Unbeknownst to me because remember this is the first time I touched him, his dick was fucking huge. I pretended to be stroking him but instead I was using the circle of my fingers to grasp and slide from the tip to the base. From what I could discern, at its widest, my hand circle separated to allow about ¾ inch between my fingers and not to mention, at least 10 inches long. FUCK!

Randy didn't need any help with his rock-hard guide. I needed fucking help at the entrance of this ride. So, after my careful measuring expedition, I refocused on myself. Excitement and panic showed up at the same time. My heart and nerves started with their co-op efforts to get every part of me to relax. I reached down to re-examine the degree of wetness with which he would be working. I mean it's wet but, hell, I need a torrential downpour. I used my right

75

hand to aid the downpour and my left hand to continue stroking the guide. As I was doing so, I was rubbing the tip of Randy's dick along my vaginal entrance. He loved that shit, all the while holding himself slightly elevated. I could feel my sweetness flowing. The room became heady with the scent of my sex. So, now I'm ready. I placed his dick at the entrance, shifted my hips, and used the fingers of both hands to hold open the lips on each side to widen the entrance. Ironically, now Randy waited. He was probably used to this moment.

I'm open, every part of me participating in this effort. Randy is just inside. He starts pushing his hips forward. He's gentle as fuck. He pushes. I widen. He pushes some more. I widen some more. He pulls back. I relax. On the next push forward, he reaches down to move my arms. I could hear him swallow. I used my hands to grasp his arms. It's time to hold on. My body took over once it realized that we were actually taking this giant dick. Panic left. I could feel my body heating up. My hips became brave. My love sounds escaped my mouth. My breathing kept reminding me of the force within me. It didn't take long for me to feel the blood racing to orgasm central. I tried to slow it down but Randy was in an amazing rhythm. He was so strong. Slowly but firmly he penetrated out and in and on the in stroke, he did this little grind motion. He repeated that movement. He moaned. I moaned.

I'm no longer aware of my participation. I'm taking and giving and then all of a sudden, my body is in full blow spasms under this man. He digs deep and holds his body still while I completed my convulsions. Relief washed over me. I'm not sure what caused him to start back his motion. I do know that once I was done I was done. Just like that, I'm ready to go. As I'm lying under him motionless, I'm sure Randy believes he is making sweet love to me. I'm staring at the ceiling. I'm waiting for him to finish. At some point, he finished.

He offered to take me back to my hotel. I told him that I would get a car. I thanked him for a great evening. He looked at me and said, "You never gave me a chance." I replied "a chance to what?" He said, "To show you that I could be genuine and love you." I smiled and replied, "We had a great time." He looked me straight in my eyes and said, "I had a great time, you obliged me." Before I could say anything, he added, "I guess I should've waited on you to call me." I smiled from a distant place and headed outside to wait for my car.

Beauty:

the qualities in a person or a thing that give pleasure to the senses or the mind

Prince died on this day.

I had gone to dinner with a gentleman friend, let's call him Alex. Kind of a date, kind of a hang-out... We had experienced each other sexually but it was not the nature of our 'thing.' We have said, "I love you" to each other maybe we do maybe we don't. I mean on some level, I'm sure we do. In a nutshell, he was available to hang out and, at this time, I needed to be with someone who wanted to be with me. He was wild, fun, and pretty darn good looking too.

Alex and I had a friend in common, Ian, who always hand a party or kick-back going on at his crib. So, after the devastating news of the death of Prince and a nice sushi dinner, we decided to call upon our friend to see if he were hosting the mourning services at his home. Well, in true Ian fashion, he said, "Of course, grab a bottle, come through." Alex and I were like "cool" see you in a bit. As we headed to the package store, Alex reminded me of the location of Ian's home. He added, "But he has plenty of room, so if we drink too much, we can crash there for the night." My response was "Cool, let's do it." I believe we picked up a 12-pack of beer, Jack Daniels which is Ian's favorite and of course, my favorite gluten-free vodka, Tito's. Then we hit the road.

Upon arrival, it was just the three of us, Ian, Alex and me. We sat around the table as we sipped on our drinks, snacked on chips or something and talked. Funny, I remember Alex lowering his head whenever he walked through the dining area to avoid hitting his head on the chandelier, he's pretty tall. Ian is taller than me but the height of the chandelier didn't bother either of us. After a few near misses of fucking up his head, Alex was like, "Hey man, no disrespect, but do you mind if I make a few minor adjustments, I'm about to kill myself in this bitch." Well, Ian shrugged his shoulders and stood up, then Alex came to my chair to pull it back, prompting me to stand so now we are all standing, Ian and I are looking at Alex like "ok what now?" Alex moves the table over about 2 feet centered under the chandelier. Ian and I looked at each other again, shook our heads and I believe he said something like "tall people problems." Alex made a comment about living to see another day. We all laughed. It was good, that's exactly how it was when we were together. Good.

As time passed, others began to arrive, as if on cue but randomly. I believed Ian's home contained a magnetic pull that drew people from all over. After getting to know Ian, I found out it's him. People love to be around him. He's cool as fuck, easy-going, warm, open, sexy and, well...comfortable. I used to tease him about having a harem; in private conversations, I would call him 'Sultan.' I wasn't sure if the ladies of his harem were aware that they were a part of such an elite group. There were always beautiful women around. Tonight, was not going to be any different. Starting with me...

Of course, Reader, you know, I'm always lost in the time. When I'm enveloped in a warm, loving safe space, it's totally forgotten....

Someone asked a question, loudly, which gained all of our attention... "What's your favorite Prince song?" That's how we started our tribute to Prince. Everyone started to answer, some laughed and some were crying. We were all talking at the same time to whomever could hear us.

It was during this conversation that I realized that I had been staring at this woman across the table from me. So, I sat there for a second like, "How long have you been looking at her?" I knew her name but I didn't know her. We had crossed paths a couple of times, probably here or someplace else. "Have I ever noticed her?" So, the conversation is circling around me because I'm seriously caught in this woman's aura and having a conversation with my damn self. Alex interrupted my revelry, "Hey Babe, you good? Wanna hit this?" I nodded, yes to both. I was good. I took a hit. He followed up, "Want me to get you another drink?" Yes, again. The whole time my eyes continued to drift back to her, Lilli.

Lilli, no e. Lilli is beautiful. She's the most genuine representation of a woman that I had ever seen. Ok, now that thought alone should let you know that I was feeling some kind of way. Let me try to describe her, I'm not going to point out what she wasn't, only focusing on what she was. Her breasts were free under her black blouse. Dark areolas, could I see them? Am I just imagining them from the outline? The skin leading from her neck to her chest area glistened. I was looking, thinking, "Is that perspiration?" Nah, the temperature is comfortable in here, maybe it's flakes of gold in her complexion and they are reflecting the light from the chandelier. I could agree with that, so I did...gold. Lilli's hair was locked, shoulder length, slightly darker than her skin, some funky twist design. I wanted to touch it, I thought, "Have I ever touched locks before?" I remembered yeah, I have. I wonder if hers feel different. She's conversing with the guy next to her. I'm watching. Is she moving in slow motion? He said something. Her face changed, became stern, I saw her mouth the word "no" and she continued to stare at him. I was instantly mad at him. How could he upset her? What did he say? He said something else to her as another lady approached. Lilli turned to face her. They were friends. I could tell because space didn't exist between them. I sipped my drink and watched.

Lilli stood. She and her friend girl moved into the kitchen as if to have a private conversation. Looking back, I probably seemed anti-social to everyone because mentally I was completely absent. I'm sitting and breathing, trying to get it together. It's like I'm in a trance. I stayed. There's no harm in the air. I'm going to enjoy the trance. Ian must have been watching me watch Lilli. He entered my space, I felt him,

82

his energy is huge, but mainly because he was saying my name as he did. "Joy, hey babe, you good?" I blink a couple of times, shook my shoulders, inhaled and exhaled quickly, then replied, "I don't know, Sweet Sultan" and laughed. He smiled and continued, "Do you need anything?" He held out a blunt, I took it. "Nah, I'm fine. I'll refresh my drink in a moment." He said, "Let me get that for you." I smiled at him because in that moment, I realize that I love him. Hell, I probably loved everybody, in this moment.

My eyes are drawn to the corner of the kitchen. Lilli and her friend are chatting and laughing. Lilli was sitting on the counter leaning up against the refrigerator. Relaxed. Open. Her friend was standing languidly next to her. Totally, a girlfriend moment, I recognized it. Everyone ceases to exist when best girlfriends are together. She's wearing a skirt, hmm, I didn't notice that before. Her feet are bare. She's wearing a silver anklet. It's funny, with as much as I remember about her, I can't recall the color of her toenails. Ian came back with my drink. I thanked him. I thought to myself "where's Alex?" I scanned the room. I forgot that I was looking for him because when I looked back into the kitchen, Lilli was looking at me. I inhaled deeply. She held my eyes; after what seemed like an eternity, she smiled. I smiled back, I think. Ian, still standing there, whispered "she's magic." I turned to look him deep in his eyes and then he added "but so are you." His comment caught me off guard. Impulsively, I asked, "Sweet Sultan, will you please take my shoes off?" I'm not sure why, I guess I needed something to be unrestricted. Why not start with my toes? He didn't say anything, I turned in my chair facing him, and he kneeled down to remove my shoes, patiently, right shoe, left shoe. He stood up and said, "you have beautiful feet." I smiled in appreciation. I turned back around to the table, Ian walked off with my shoes in his hands.

I'm alone again. I still don't know where Alex is but that's ok, this feels like home...safe, I reminded myself. I remember looking down at the table, spending way too much mental energy trying to come up with shapes within the design of the marble. I was trying to decide if I should look up again, because I know my only reason for doing so will be to look at her...Lilli. So, I give in to the pull of her energy, I raise my head and slowly began to lift my eyes to find the source of my immediate desires. There she was, laughing. She tossed her head back, still laughing. My mind was leaving without me. "How does she smell?" Let's go see. "What does her skin tastes like?" Let's go see. "Will she be offended if I touch her?" Let's go see.

She turned ever so slightly and looked at me. I didn't look away. I smiled. She smiled then waved her hand, telling me to come into the kitchen. My mind was cheering but my brain was trying to figure out the best possible route to walk 10 feet and if we could indeed walk 10 feet and where are my shoes and what will we say when we get there. So, finally they, my mind and brain, are trying to work together. I smiled and nodded my head as if to say 'ok.' At which point, I stood up and began my initial trek to get closer to Lilli's magic. I notice Alex out of the corner of my eye, he's watching me. I felt like I was gliding. I wonder if it looks like that to him.

My body stops moving. I'm here. I made it. I lift my glass for a toast, they both raised theirs, I said, "Cheer's to the legacy of Prince and to magic, everywhere." "Cheers." "Here, here to the magic." We laughed together. Lilli's friend spoke first; she reached up to twirl my hair. I lowered my face and blushed. She said, "I love your hair, how long have you been natural?" I replied, "A year or so and I absolutely love it." She said something like "I know what you mean; I locked my hair about five years ago. The best decision I ever made. I mean until it's time to do something different." We laughed. As I'm standing there, it dawns on me Lilli's friend is carrying the conversation because they are reading my energy. Ha! I'm in a trap. They are trying to feel me. Hmm ok, I see. If that's the case, check this out, I took a step closer to both of them, closing the gap. This boldness just shows up when-the-fuck-ever. They felt me because they both inhaled. I just stood there as we continued to talk. Well, they weren't uncomfortable with the closeness because neither of them moved. I wasn't either; I actually wanted to be closer, closer to, surprisingly, both of them.

Lilli speaks, "Why were you sitting alone?" I wasn't quite sure how to respond, so my mind took over and blurted out, "It was by choice. I was watching you. I was enjoying watching you." By the end, my words slowed to a soft, barely audible coo. Lilli laughed. "Thank you" she said and added "I was watching you too." For a brief moment I was speechless, I stood there and then I said, "May I touch your hair?" She leaned forward; I reached up to touch her hair. I don't know what I expected but it felt nice, I guess. So, I'm touching her hair and I realize that her friend is still twirling in mine. I can feel saliva filling my mouth. I swallowed. I realize that I'm tipsy or high or both. I'm not responding as myself but as someone who looks like me and lives in me. It feels good, right.

The three of us are all in this moment, when Alex approaches and says, "Hey Baby, you good?" I close my eyes, swallow and look up to meet Lilli's eyes. She nodded 'yes'. I didn't even turn to look at him, I just answered "yes." He said, "Alright then, I'll be right over there" and walked off. After a few moments, I asked Lilli, can I kiss you? Her body answered, she moved forward to get down, I stepped back to allow her space. With her left hand she grabbed her friend's right hand; the low movement caught my attention. It was then I considered that I may be given the pleasure of kissing them both. I felt my body getting warmer with that thought. Lilli took her right hand and reached up for my face, I almost fainted at the softness of her hand against my skin, my eyes closed and my lips parted. Then I felt them, her breasts pressing against mine, I wanted to remove my dress and my bra to feel her nakedness. Instead, I was distracted by her lips... those full, sensual, moist lips. I drank from her lips. I used my tongue to search for words, thoughts anything that she held there. She tasted so good. I bit her bottom lip a little. As a show of appreciation, she bit mine back. I moaned, my neck relaxed and my head rolled back. She held my lip between her teeth. Her friend reached for my head, maybe she thought it would disconnect from my body. I helped her to raise it, Lilli released my lip. As soon as she released my lip, her friend planted her lips on mine. She opened my lips wider with her tongue then she explored my mouth, possibly trying to salvage what was left of my kiss with Lilli. I was helpless and weak.

Noises, talking, music, oh shit I forgot about the other people there! No one joined us, no one interrupted, and those who watched, watched from the perimeter of the kitchen. We stayed there kissing, they were alternating kissing me; though, I never saw them kiss each other. This kissing session lasted for what seems like forever. Y'all know how I am about keeping track of time. This was sheer ecstasy and I was lost in it.

Alex and Ian came into the kitchen. Ian grabbed the attention of Lilli and her friend. Alex was like "Hey Baby, let me talk to you for a minute. Walk this way." He reached for my hand and I followed. We went into the bathroom; he closed the door and said, "You know those women aren't just gonna kiss you all night right? They are gonna be trying to lick your pussy and shit. Are you good with that?" Dazed, I was like "what?" Well, Alex proceeded to repeat his previous statement and question. I said "Uh, I don't know." He just looked at me for a moment. He was trying to read my thoughts but I didn't have any. I was trying to get back to the magic. Why was he doing this? What the fuck? As I'm standing there ranting at him in my head. He's just watching me. My immediate reality is that I had to pee. I said, "I have to pee." He said "pee." I took a deep breath, realizing that he wasn't leaving me alone. I pulled down my panties which were wet with my desires. After I finished, I stood up, washed my hands and standing there looking in the mirror, I caught Alex's eyes watching me. I was high as fuck. I said aloud "I'm fucked-up." He said, "I know Baby." All of a sudden, I'm nervous and aware. I turned to look at Alex; I said, "I need to go to bed." He said "come on." I followed obediently.

We walked through the house; I was desperately trying to catch a glimpse, only if fleeting, at Lilli. She was gone. Her friend was gone. We kept walking. At the top of the stairs, Alex pointed to the first room on the right "Sleep in here." I said, "What if someone comes in here?" He said, "No one is coming in here." I asked, "Is there another room, somewhere further away from the stairs?" He pointed with his head to the room further down the hall on the left. I walked to that room. The door was closed. As I put my hand on the doorknob, Alex said, "But they are eating pussy in there." Lilli...I inhaled deeply, closed my eyes, and placed my head on the door, thinking... I stayed there possibly trying to inhale her scent through the door, I wanted to hear her love sounds, I wanted to be lost in the sea of her legs, lips and tongue but... for whatever reason, I couldn't turn the knob.

I looked back down the hall. Alex stood by the first door waiting. He was looking at me patiently with understanding. I walked back to him and he led me to the bed. I got in bed completely dressed. He covered me with comforter. He kissed me on the head and left. I didn't have a last thought before I drifted off to sleep. The next morning, I woke up in a panic. Where was I? Why was I here? Who's in the bed with me? I looked, it was Alex. My panic began to subside. I felt my body to make sure I was still clothed, I was. I watched Alex sleep for a few minutes before I woke him. Damn, I appreciate this n-word. He was the truth last night. I'll have to remember to thank him for taking care of me.

Alex is awake now. He's gotta get to work. As I sit up, I start to think "Where are my shoes and my purse?" I looked around, over there on the chair hung my purse with my shoes neatly placed on the floor beside it. Alex and I leave quietly. We drive in silence for most of the way. He said, "Did you have fun last night?" I laughed "yyeeesss! I was too turned on." He said "Yeah I know!" He continued with "I know you were high as hell. When I saw you watching Lilli, I said Let me keep an eye on my baby before Lilli turns her the-fuck-out." We laughed. I said "Thanks Alex." He said, "it's cool. You know, I love your naive ass." Hmph, I smiled, "I love you too."

Generosity:

*the quality of being kind, understanding,
and not selfish*

I awoke amorous today. As I think about it, it was like most days; though, for some reason, it felt slightly different; I'm not talking about the feeling of sexual desire. Nah, that wasn't different; in fact, that feeling is pretty common these days. 'It' is referring to the warm, moist, silky area on that piece of flesh at the vaginal entrance. It's one of my favorite places to touch; it's like taking my pulse when I'm considering pleasuring myself.

Well this morning, I'm still lying in bed contemplating, to cum or not to cum? Not much of a dilemma I guess but whatever, it was currently my most pressing issue. As I'm tossing this idea around, I'm using my index finger to transfer the silky feeling from my favorite place to my brain. It's usually during this time that a little alarm sounds to alert my nerves and blood cells that there's going to be a pretty explosive meeting at an area nearby. But not this morning, every part of my body, including my mind was relaxed; though, my silky place remains loyal. Even in downtimes... it remains warm, moist and yes, silky. I guess I'll have to be content with the pleasurable smell, taste and feeling derived from my finger excursion.

I willed myself to get up, so aloud I said, "Alright Chickie time to get up. Rise and shine." As with any other morning, I have to have some music. Pandora on. Blinds open. What a beautiful day? Just like that, I'm ready to start this day. As I'm leaving the restroom, my phone rings... I already know who it is, one of my best girlfriends, Kendall, she works from home on most days. Her schedule is hella flexible. So, we talk often and randomly throughout the day. I answered. After the necessary hellos and health checks, Kendall tells me she's working on something... my curiosity is piqued and I'm listening because we always have a great time.

Kendall: "So I talked to 'dude' last night. He's talking about picking up some beer and a bushel of oysters."

90

Note: Kendall refers to all guys as 'dude.' It's funny 'cause names don't mean anything to her. She's an energy person. So, if she enjoys your presence, she'll probably start using a term of endearment, like 'babe'; Otherwise, it's dude until she picks up on an energy change or until they go away.

Me: "How much fun is that gonna be! Raw oysters?"

Kendall: "Nah, not raw."

She goes on to talk about the various ways to process and cook oysters. I have her on speaker phone, so as she's talking, I'm going about my daily routine of getting dressed.

I said something like, "Oh I didn't know that...," Kendall continued her thought.

Me: "Hilarious! That'll be great."

Kendall: "What time are you off? Can you come? There will be other people there."

Me: "Probably around 3pm. Girl, you know it'll take me a couple of hours to get to the Atlanta area though. But, yeah, I'd love to come."

Now, I have a little more spring in my step. Plans... I love when plans are being made.

Kendall: "That's perfect because I'm going right after work. We may get there about the same time."

Me: "Do you know if any single men are gonna be there? I'm horny as fuck."

Kendall: "I don't know but I'm sure if you let someone, single or married, know you are trying to hook up, they will hook up."

We laughed.

Me: "Girl, that's the truth! Anyway, when you get there scan the crowd. Let me know what you see and send me a text me. Hell, I may need to turn around."

Kendall laughed and said, "I got you."

We end our call with a "be safe and see you later." Then I say, "I love you."

Now, I'm dancing around my room. I love having plans, something for which to look forward. I mean you know it's gonna be good, right? Especially since, no one ever plans to have a "bad" time. My focus changed from getting dressed now to what I'll wear tonight. I laugh to myself. Damn, do I have clothes in my suitcase to wear to an oyster boil or bake or kick-back? I'll figure it out later. Let me get this workday over. Singing in my head, "I've got plans tonight!"

By day's end, I've decided that I'm wearing black leggings, short-sleeved ocelot print knit shirt, and black ankle boots...my oyster shucking outfit! I hit the road right after work. I was completely turned up singing in my head "ATL hoe!"

What the fuck? This traffic, ughhh! ATL hhoooeee!

I send a text.

Me: "I'm close Chick. Stopping to change clothes and grab beer."

Kendall: "Cool."

Me: "How are we looking?"

Kendall: "Come on through..."

Yes, my girl, she has given the crowd a once over. So, hurriedly I change clothes, wash my face, reapply my mascara and gloss my lips. I look in the mirror. Playtime bitches! I throw myself a kiss and head-out into the store. I walked directly to the beer cooler. Scanning looking for my favorite beer...yes, I select Stella for me and Bud light for everyone else. I grabbed a 12-pack of each and head for the check-out counter. Oooh chocolates let me grab a couple... I ask the clerk "How much for these?" He replied, nonchalantly "fitty nine cents." I smile because I know he answers that same question at least a hundred times a week. I said "cool" and grabbed four. Paid for my purchase, with my bag on my shoulder, chocolates in my purse, a 12-pack in each hand, I left the store. Playtime bitches!

Once in the car, I drove about 15 more minutes to "dude's" place. Hmph I silently thanked my GPS for great directions, I found the apartment without a single hitch. I grabbed my purse, always a cross-body bag, one of my little quirks. I need to have my hands free. I retrieved the beer, a package in each hand and headed for the door. I knocked with my knee. A guy opened the door; I quickly scanned the room from outside the door, searching for Kendall. Bingo! There she is. I stepped in "Hey everyone" and I looked at the door opener, smiled and said "thank you." Kendall and dude walked over. I raised the beer. He said "perfect! I love Bud light." I laughed and thought "good." He took the beer from my hands. Kendall and I hugged. She introduced us, I don't remember his name but he was good looking. I didn't have to remember because Kendall said, "Babe this is J." Babe? Oh yeah she is feeling him. After that intro, his name didn't even matter. I follow them into the kitchen. I'm walking smiling, saying hi to the other guests, checking faces, who's in this room for me? I'm guessing that there were about 10 people or so, I lost count at seven. There was no reason to count anyone else beyond the number seven.

I got his name later but for now, let's call him Seven. Lucky number Seven...we saw each other. I heard Kendall say "J you want a Stella or Tito's?" I kept looking at Seven. I said, "Gimme a second, I'm going to have some chocolate first." I guess she looked to see that Seven and I had each other's attention because she said, "Oh ok, well I'm pouring you a shot of Tito's." I reached into my purse to pull out a chocolate square. I never took my eyes off Seven. I opened the chocolate, held it up and said to him, "Would you like to share this with me?" His smile was slight. He moved forward to fill the space between us. Well, when he was close enough, I took the chocolate square and inserted half of it in my mouth, my teeth holding it in place to allow his half to stick out. I notice that he's not much taller than me, a couple or three inches maybe. His skin is the same complexion as this chocolate that's starting to melt against my tongue. It's warm and sweet. I wonder if he tastes the same. He's standing in front of me in my space. He feels good in it. But he hasn't taken his half of the chocolate. So, of course, I start thinking... Is this too much? Should I break it and let him take his share? Well, I lifted my head to alter my view. It was then that he leaned in to get his chocolate. He was waiting for me to lift it to him as an offering. By now, the piece on my tongue was melting and thick mixing with my saliva.

Seven opened his mouth. Instinctively, my eyes closed. I felt his lips touch mine, my expectation was that he would bite his chocolate and step back. I mean, what should I expect of a stranger to whom I have offered to share a piece of chocolate out of my mouth? Well, he bit his piece but he didn't move, turns out he wanted my half too. He continued. He must really like chocolate. He licked the chocolate residue from between and on my teeth. I let him have it. He wanted more. So I opened wide and allowed him to get all he could get from the depths of my mouth. I didn't tell him that I had more chocolate in my purse. I wanted him to continue to explore my mouth looking for more. Unprompted, I reached up to place my arms around his neck; he responded by enveloping me in his arms. Our chocolate mission has turned into passion. This kiss was the sweetest, softest form of an introduction. I became aware before he did. I heard Kendall's Babe say, "Do they know each other?" She said, "I don't think so, but they will."

I didn't move but I lowered my eyes and attempted to change the position of my arms. Seven pulled me closer. He wanted my arms to stay. I put them back and looked into his face. We haven't said hi "yet" and we still didn't. "Hi" wasn't enough of a greeting for this moment. My body is awake. I felt my nipples pressing at the t-shirt and thought "I should've worn a bra." Reading my mind, he loosened his grip, freed one of his hands, then effortlessly slid it under my t-shirt and rubbed his thumb across my nipple. I inhaled deeply and my eyes rolled in response. I could feel his hardness pressing against my thigh. Breathe. I felt like I couldn't get enough air. He started breathing with me, guiding me. Calming me.

I don't believe that either of us knew what was going on. Maybe I was at an advantage because this morning when I awoke I knew that I needed something more than the pleasure of my own fingers to assist in the release of this pent up energy. Hmm with that thought, correction, I do know what's going on. I'm placing myself on the altar for his taking. Let me show him. While looking in his eyes, I press my body into his, I reposition my hand on his neck, holding it firmly, I part my lips and lean in to kiss him... hard and hungrily. I had to show him that I wanted to give myself to him. He responded by removing my hand from his neck and forcefully pushing it along with my arm behind my back. He held it there and returned the hungry, but harder, kiss. He was showing me that he was in charge of this moment. Fuck it, that's cool with me. Take me.

Keep in mind, we are in an apartment with several people. Music is playing. Laughter and conversations, oysters are being shucked. Regular house-party shit is happening all around us. Seven and I are oblivious to all of it. Nothing exists but the time and space within us. He starts walking forward still holding my arm behind my back. I hold onto him tighter with my free arm to keep from falling. So, he's walking forward that means I'm walking backwards and kissing at the same damn time. We stop, I feel something pressing against my calf. Is that a couch? It was a convertible air sofa bed. I don't know the correct name but it seems like a piece of furniture acquired for a bachelor's first apartment. Seven turns us around, he sits on the sofa bed thing and pulls my arm for me to follow. I do. I lay on him, his legs are open and my legs are together between his. More kissing, more touching, my body is pressing against his. Oh my Lord, thank you for gravity, pressure, force, everything responsible for allowing me to feel this man underneath me. My legs wanted to open. I couldn't stop them. One at a time they parted ways, to straddle this man; I could feel his dick pressing against my pussy. I struggle with that word, uuughhh but in this moment it is apropos. I've straddled him, we are kissing, I'm grinding my pussy through my leggings into his jeans. I wanted this man to fuck me right now but not right here in this open space of people. Well because my body loves itself, it began to work on releasing this orgasm. Slow grinding, rocking, kissing with Seven, I could feel it, faster, I moan, "I'm gonna to cum." Seven took his hands and held my hips place. He stopped my explosion. Hell, I no longer cared who was in the room, this mission was selfish or...so I thought. He kinda moved so that I would roll off him and I did. He moved to floor on his knees in front of me. He reached up under my t-shirt, grabbed my leggings at the waist and began to pull them down. I placed my heeled boot firmly on the ground and raised my hips. So, now I'm on the air thing, leggings at my knees and my boots are still on. Seven raises my legs and enters under them; he's designed his own trap with my leggings holding him

96

in place. I can feel his breath against the hot wetness, it should've been a cooling effect but I was getting hotter and wetter. Seven must be a mind reader because the first thing he did was spread my lips and lick my favorite place, that silky piece that lines the entrance. Just like that I let out a moan that quieted the room; my body started convulsing and released my first orgasm. I was dazed. Seven didn't move, he didn't change the position of his body or his mouth. He continued to lick and play in that area. He was waiting for my juicy sweetness to flow to him. He wanted an instant replay. I didn't rush him; he has already shown me that he's in control of this moment. I just stayed in position and tried not to make eye contact with anyone.

Kendall brought me the shot she was saving for me. She and I took a shot. She left me with a bottle of water. With that, a couple of other people came over to make things more comfortable for Seven while he was exploring his prize. Let's see, I remember in between moans someone removed my boots. My leggings were removed, which freed Seven from his self-made trap. When that happened he sat back on his haunches, unbuckled his belt, unbuttoned and unzipped his pants. He stood up on his knees pulled his pants and boxers down. I sat up. I wanted to suck his dick. He didn't say anything. He put his hand on my chest and pushed me back on the air sofa. He grabbed my hips and pulled me to the edge of the sofa. He took his hands and spread my legs at the knees. He looked blankly at my pussy. He took his fingers and spread my thighs, holding my lips and ass cheeks open. I don't know what he was thinking. I placed myself on the altar for him, now I'm at his mercy. Finally, he moved his hands, he had made a decision and he moved his body closer. He was so close that his pubic arch was touching my lips. My anticipation was growing, breathe, he inched back until he made room between us for his dick. When he touched himself, I imagined it was my hand. How did it feel? How does it look? Is it hot? Is it heavy? I wanted to feel the blood filling him to course through my hand. Seven grabbed his dick; in response

I opened my legs wider, I was ready. He began to move forward, I was open. I could feel his heat before he entered me. I took a deep breath preparing my mind and body for whatever power he was capable of delivering. Exhale. He's filling my openness. I'm holding my breath. He's in. He stops. We are both lost in the pleasure, enjoying the throbbing that each of our bodies are emitting. The sensations became so entwined that our pulses were in harmony, the resounding effect was so loud. Slowly, he moved his hands to my knees. He pushed them open. He wanted me wider. I obliged. He began to move his hips, back, forth, back and forth. He was wherever men go in their minds when caught in the rapture. I was completely engulfed in the waves of ecstasy that continued to wash over me. I could feel my hips moving desperately trying to meet his thrusts. My instincts took over, I was meeting him, harder, faster, and deeper, I wanted everything he was giving. He was taking everything that I laid before him. My nerves and blood cells, my biggest cheerleaders, were screaming "Yes, Joy this is it, give it to him, yes, yes." Hell, how could I not comply? With my eyes closed and my mind black, my body was functioning on its own. I could feel my orgasm preparing to make its dramatic exit. I said it aloud, telling no one in particular, "I'm cumming." Seven took that as his cue assist more in this effort. By that time, his assistance was no longer needed. Through a series electric shocks, my orgasm had arrived. I just laid there, it was not time to recover. So, I didn't try. No words were needed. Every sound around us combined and resembled black noise.

Seven slowed his stroke to a long slow motion. He attempted to keep me alive. I moaned, signaling there was still life in me. He touched my neck, gently at first then as if losing himself, he grabbed my neck tighter. I couldn't tell if he were trying to choke me or hold on while he rode his own powerful wave. It seemed like he wasn't getting inside of me enough to satisfy his needs. He kept trying to go deeper; maybe he wanted his whole body inside. I laid there and took it, too

98

exhausted to counter his beast. Suddenly, he pulled out and at the same time pulled me to a sitting position with the hand that held my neck. Immediately I realized what he was taking next. He wanted my mouth, the place from his earlier expedition. He was erect and covered in my sweetness. I leaned forward, to start his ending process. I couldn't suck easy, he was ready to finish and I was focused on getting him there. I drew him into my mouth like a vacuum, I sucked feverishly, I stroked and sucked over and over. Now he was helpless, I was the taker. After a few moments, I felt his body stiffen. He buried his hands in my hair, holding on. His body was tense and mouth was silent as he came in my mouth.

His cum was delicious; thick, salty and sweet and filled the hollow of my mouth. When he realized that he was still holding my hair, he slowly released it and began straightening it like he was apologizing for his destruction. He lifted my head to meet his gaze. I lifted my eyes to him and swallowed. Something, I could not recognize, flashed through his eyes. He smiled a gentle smile. I think that once he realized there were still people there, he tried to cover me. He didn't want them to see me unclothed. It's a fine damn time for that! I slipped on my leggings. We kept looking at each trying to figure out what the fuck just happened. Comments were made by the other guests, like "Is there any chocolate left?" and "Are y'all sure y'all didn't know each other?"

After we were dressed, Seven said, "I'd like to spend more time with you. Would you like to join me for a drink?" I said, "Yes, I'd love a drink, by the way, I'm Joy." He told me his name but I forgot as soon as he said it. For the rest of the night, I called him "Sweetness." Each time he answered.

We finally joined the oyster-shucking party. He and I had a great time. I was happy that Kendall invited me. As people started leaving, he and I had figured out how to convert the air sofa into an airbed. That's where we played all night. Me and Seven exploring each other's everything. When I awoke the following morning, quietly I was collecting my things. Kendall was still here, I saw her shoes. I'll text her later. Seven opened his eyes. He said, "Leave me your number." I smiled and replied, "Sweetness, that's not necessary. Let's keep our time great." I placed a chocolate where I slept, blew him a kiss and left.

Patience:

the ability to wait for a long time without becoming annoyed or upset

Last night, I took a bath, a long, lingering, steamy hot bath...

Funny, because, I rarely spend time actually taking a sit-down bath. I don't know why, time consuming, showering is more convenient, hmm not really sure but I have to say that I thoroughly enjoyed it!

As I'm sitting here thinking about it, trying to gather the words to paint a picture for the reader of this entry, the first thing I need to correct is the opening statement...

Here goes, last night, a bath was drawn, steamy and hot then my beautiful, towering man guest bathed me... Before I get into the details, let me paint his picture... Anyone who knows me know that I love, love, love big men. I don't even have an answer as to why, I just do. For the sake of continuing this entry AND anonymity, let's call him Ghost. He has to have a name. Now, I'm laughing to myself because the diminutive, Ghost, fits him. He's about 6'4, possibly 300lbs he actually mentioned that he has put on a few pounds, here lately. Perfect! His skin is like a creamy dark chocolate, he has a strong jaw bone with kind eyes, he's wearing his head shaved with a kick-ass, salt and pepper beard.

Some background, Ghost and I met at an event years ago... He saw me, I saw him, we started trying to figure it out without even speaking a word. When we got close enough to each other, brief conversation ensued. I told him to come to my room that, unfortunately, I was sharing with hella chicks. Honestly, I wanted to get him alone, to hold his dick in my hand and possibly feel it on my lips. Now, he didn't know this, he might have hoped for something like it but he didn't know what was on my mind. Once, I got him to the room, we had to go into the bathroom (if the other couple that was in the bathroom with us is reading this, this is your shout-out)! Ghost looked at me, I took his hand and pulled him with me, I sat down on the toilet, seat

102

lid down, kinda motioned for him to come closer, he obliged. I looked up at his face, as he was still standing and I proceeded to unbuckle his belt. Admittedly, he was thrown off. He was looking back at the other couple and then down at me. All the while, I never took my eyes off of his face. Finally, I had his belt unbuckled, his pants unfastened and unzipped, his fly open on his boxers and my hand inside holding his dick. Full, thick, heavy, warm dick. I promise you my mouth started watering. So, I'm looking at him, we have some serious eye contact now. Hell, I believe we both forgot there were other people in the bathroom with us. Too funny. I'm waiting on a nod or something in his face to give me silent permission to unveil this prize. Then it happened he moved ever so slightly, almost as he were making room for his dick to make an entrance. By now, of course, it's rock hard, bulging, throbbing, and hot in my hand. I tried to pull it through the boxers but I couldn't, too anxious, maybe... With his left hand, he gently removed my hand from the boxer opening and continued holding me at my wrist. While he pulled his boxers down with his right hand, this beautiful, oh so, beautiful dick made his grand entrance. The sight of it, literally, took my breath away. He then placed my hand, of the wrist he was holding, within reach. After I looked at it, touched it to my nose, just to inhale his maleness, rubbed it across my lips, I opened my mouth, inserted his dick and began a slow, powerful sucking motion! Did I mention already that I didn't know him from Adam? I was, obviously, out of my mind. So, as I'm sucking his dick, I mean good too, like I'm trying to draw the essence of him inside of me, I noticed movement out of the corner of my eye. People are standing at the door watching me suck his dick... Ok, right, now I'm aware and embarrassed, I came to my fucking senses... I asked myself, am I honestly sucking this man's dick with an audience? I looked at him, he looks as if caught between 'please don't stop' and 'is this a problem?' I'm too tickled thinking about that night...

At my suggestion, we fixed ourselves, even as the audience protested. As we left, he said, "Let me get your number?" I gave it to him. When we parted ways, he said, "What's your name?" I was so fucking embarrassed that I just kept walking. Anyway, as chance meetings go, we texted a bit. We even crossed paths at a few events. He finally got the nerve to ask again, "What's your name?" He said, "I've had you saved as 'The One' since that night." I giggled and then gave him my real name... Joy.

All of that background, so that we can talk about "The Bath..."

I was on a flight coming into Atlanta on a Saturday. For whatever reason, Ghost crossed my mind. I haven't seen or talked to him in a year easy. Well, once my plane touched ground, I sent him a text, as soon as I took my iPhone off airplane mode.

Pretty simple text:

Me: "Hi. What's going on?"

Ghost: "Nothin', sitting here, chilling."

Ghost: "What you up to?"

Me: "I'm gonna have a drink..."

Ghost: "Where are you? Who's with you?"

Me: "I'm near the airport. I'm alone..."

Minutes passed, fucking crickets....

Me: "I'd like for you to come give me a bath."

Ghost: "Ok."

104

Ghost: "Send me the address, I'll be there in an hour."

And that dear friends is how the evening began. Of course, I went downstairs to the hotel restaurant to have dinner and drinks before his arrival. Surprisingly, I wasn't even nervous. It was if I had had a personal bather my whole life. I did, however, spend some time conjuring up his imagine. I wondered about his looks... How did he smell? Oh my goodness, I surely hope his dick is as thick as I remember. You know the mind can be quite creative...

Text message:

Ghost: "15 minutes away..."

Ghost: "Need anything?"

Me: "Vodka would be nice."

Ghost: "Got it."

Me: "553"

Me: "See you soon."

Just as I finished dinner, he called.

Ghost: "Hey, I'm here. What's up with the parking?"

Me: "I don't know. I rode the shuttle."

Ghost: "That's cool. I'll figure it out. See you in a few."

Honestly, at this point, I don't even remember the next 15 minutes. I was in a serious chill mode. Ghost was on his way ...

Pandora playing. Feeling good after my dinner and cocktails. Lips, wet and glossed. Hair, wild and free. I thought about jumping in the shower a hundred times. Hilarious! No need for that. I'm about to be given a bath. Don't you think he knows I'm gonna be a little dirty beforehand? But a lot dirty afterwards?

I'm in the mirror dancing to Jill Scott, when there's a knock, knock, knock at the door. "Oh Shit Chick, it's time, don't your trash talking ass panic now!" That's what I said to myself... I took a deep breath, went to the door, opened it, looked straight at Ghost's chest then lifted my eyes until they met his and in my mind said, "Hell yeah this n-word is everything!" My exterior was cool and collected though. My mouth said, "Hi Ghost." He said, "The One" then laughed a big laugh and said "It's about damned time." We hugged and laughed. He poured us drinks. I had mine straight, no rocks or chaser. His had a splash of cranberry. We sat in the sitting area of the hotel room and talked about 'who the hell knows what' and listened to music.

As if moved by an unknown force, while in mid-sentence, I stood, smiled a slight smile, excused myself to the bathroom where I proceeded to look at my face in the mirror. I believe I was searching for fear or anxiety, or for my mouth to utter an excuse, a reason to giggle and say "I was just playing, no bath for me." It wasn't there, instead my reflection was calm, cool and assured. Instead of turning away, I stared. Stared at myself, and began to undress, as if exploring the depth of my own eyes and the fullness and curves of each part of my body as if it was unveiled for the first time. I was lost in a moment of self-appreciation. As I breathed a slight sigh, at the touch of my own fingers, I noticed movement in the mirror.

It was him. Ghost! My first thought was how long had he been standing there? Laughing nervously to myself, I covered my breasts with my right arm, hand over left nipple while pressing my forearm to

106

shield the right. He just stood there, we locked eyes in the mirror. No words. No eye movement. We stared. I have no idea what either of us was thinking or even if we were thinking. Is this a staring contest? Or are we willing the other to make a move. Something moved between us, causing him to step forward. It was a force, an energy or something! I in all of my naked glory, thought he was coming to me. I inhaled a deep breath, closed my eyes and braced myself... I felt the gentle movement of the air around me and then I heard a sound, not the music lightly traveling from the front room, but a soft gurgling, pure, fresh, as the air changed slightly, I still stood untouched... what is that? Yes, oh, yes the bath water... I smiled, remembering I asked for a bath.

He left the bathroom, uttering something about coming right back. I stood there and released the makeshift cover from my breast. With a smirk and giggle, I thought, let me check the temperature of the water... it was nice, warm, wet... hell, it's water! Though, I do believe that I will increase the temperature just a bit. There now, that's just right. As I stood up, decidedly, to venture into the front room to retrieve my drink and music,

Ghost poked his head in the bathroom, voice so smooth and deep "Joy?"

I replied, "Yes, Sir?"

He asked, "Is there a knife in here?"

"Hmm, are you going to kill me with it?" I know, reader, crazy, right but we can laugh now; I was dead ass serious. Remember, I don't know this n-word.

Ghost laughed and replied, "Good one but if I were going to kill you, I wouldn't need a knife. I'm about to submerge you in a tub of hot water."

"Touché!" I laughed out loud and replied, "so very true. There should be a knife in the drawer or the pantry of the kitchenette. If not, I'll call the front desk." He left. I walked out, naked. At this point, I'm the only one thinking about my nakedness. He's in there killing a whatever with a knife...

So, mission accomplished drink in hand, music relocated closer to the tub. For whatever reason, I slipped into my wedges, it just felt right, strolled into the bedroom, gathered a couple of post bath items, lotion, oil for my hair, scarf and as an afterthought, I placed two condoms on the nightstand. I know, I know, I only asked for a bath but maybe afterwards I'll ask for a... fuck. Uh huh, don't judge me!

Ghost spoke, "You ready?"

How on God's green earth does this man keep entering my space without me feeling him? Are our energies in balance? Have we manifested an 'us' space?

I pivoted on my heels, looked at him, relaxed even more and replied, simply "yes."

I followed him into the bathroom.

As I entered the room, I noticed the light was less, dim even. Ghost had removed a couple of the bulbs. Check that shit, he's created some ambiance. Yay, you! I commented something like "Very nice. I like." At which time, he reached for my foot. Ha! He did notice the addition of the shoes. I loved it. I was having a blast in my head. Too funny. After removing both shoes, he reached a hand to help me in the tub.

108

I slowed my step when I noticed something in the tub, I inhaled and focused my eyes, I asked, "Is that lemon?" He answered "and lime." Well, alright Ghost, he is just as serious about this bath as I am!

With my hand in his, I stepped easily into the water, as if being led to a baptismal. The water wasn't even a foot deep but we both moved so gently, I guess neither one of us wanted to lose even a drop of this thoughtfully prepared and purified water. As I eased into the bath to a sitting position, Ghost kneeled by the side of the tub. Music playing... words lost between the steam, lemons, lime and our individual thoughts of how to proceed. I slid forward to lay back and relax. As I lay back, he placed a towel between my head and the wall. It was then that I realized, he was responding to me.

Yes, I know, I asked for this but hell it was my first time. I didn't know what to do but I'm a quick study.

So, I lay there, eyes closed, trying to regulate my breathing and paying close attention to the rise and fall of my chest. Ghost continued to kneel, patiently, by the tub for several minutes. As I breathed in, I lifted my right arm and placed it on the edge of the tub. As if on cue, he picked up a wash cloth, dipped it in the water and began to squeeze water from the cloth on my breasts and along the length of my exposed arm. We didn't speak another word, in a time that felt like forever...

I'm sure, in his mind, I became his favorite car or motorcycle. He squeezed lemon and lime in all of my nooks and crannies. He soaped his cloth and washed my soft pockets of flesh then he rinsed and started all over. As he washed my ears, he took great care not to wet my hair as he straightened the decorative gauge on my right. He washed each finger separately. He lifted my arms to wash the under area. I thought briefly, "Do I need a shave?" My breasts were lifted and washed underneath. He washed from my thighs to my toes and one at a time, the soles of my feet.

With my eyes still closed, I feel him coming closer, he leaned and whispered in my ear. "It's time to stand up now." I'll admit, I was light headed, dizzy, drowning, lost, dying and living within the same moment. He reached for me. We stood together. Without any words, I reached for my drink, he turned to retrieve it. I took a gulp. I had to get it together before I stepped out. I didn't believe that I could walk. When I finished the glass, I handed it to him. He turned his torso, placed the glass in its holding place. When he turned back to me, he said, "turn around, place your hands on the wall above your head and spread your legs."

He put his hands on my hips as if to brace me for this death defying transition of turning around. I breathed deeply and one step at a time, I began to turn from him losing his eyes and focusing more on his breathing. He wasn't going anywhere. No hurry. No worry.

So, here I am, my back to his front. He's standing tall now because I'm elongated using my hands to balance and the wall to keep me upright. I hear the cloth moving against the soap, I'm anxious or anticipating, I couldn't discern the difference. He's moving, I hear him, I feel his energy moving. I feel him. I inhaled deeply, his clothed hand finally touching my back. I exhaled. He washed my back with long strokes, up and down, up and down. As I was standing there, reminding myself to breathe, I realized that this process, for him, had less to do with me and more about him performing well. He's a perfectionist. My mind was finding a pattern to the wonderful motion of his back washing, up and "Oh my wait, what just happened?" I was startled by the sudden placement of his left hand on my shoulder, slightly but firmly gripping the base of my neck. Instinctively, my head turned, chin trying to connect to his strength, mouth searching for his fingers. While my mind was having a conversation with itself, "Chick, get it together." Ghost continued his bathing, up the length of my right arm, down, pausing to perform a circular cleansing to my shoulder. It took everything to keep my hands planted firmly on the wall; I wanted to touch everyplace he touched.

I could hear him rinsing the cloth in the tub, his body low, dipping the cloth in and out of the water. His face was only a couple of inches from my bottom, so close that when he stood, after re-soaping, I felt the slight brush of his beard on the skin of my butt as he stood. "Hmm had I been standing this way? Or did my back arch in anticipation? Lord, this damned brain of mine, help! Shhh," as I quieted my brain. Just as a details go, he stood and begin to wash the left arm with the same patience and attention as before.

Ok, I have no idea what's going on in his mind but I was about to fucking explode! Whew, my bath had turned into some kinda torture, I was completely turned on. This man had me on the verge of an orgasm, just by fulfilling my request for a bath. So, when I felt his hands on my hips, I was like "Yeeessss, I'm ready." He leaned in close, nudged my head with his face, as if to get me to turn my ear to him, I responded. He whispered in my ear "lift your right leg, put it here" pointing to the side of the tub. My mind was on go! "I'm not gonna make it." Aloud I said, "Oh no need for that, I can do the rest." He just stared at me. He took any power that I may have used to object, by looking deep into my soul. Without another word, I lifted my leg and placed it exactly where he wanted.

Now, picture this, I'm standing in the tub, with my left leg holding the bulk of my weight, left arm bracing against the wall, right leg lifted and resting on the outside wall of the tub, looking for a place to put my right arm, I reached up to grab the shower curtain rod. But, yikes I couldn't get comfortable. My bather, so intuitive, recognized my distress, stood up from his kneeled position on the floor, took my right arm, placed it on his left shoulder. His eyes caught the attention of mine, willing me to calm the fuck down, I guess I was messing up his process. He maintained eye contact until he was back on his knees and in position with my right arm comfortable across his shoulder.

My body is ready; my mind is questionable, as always. Ghost is soaping the cloth. By this time, the sound is soothing and cataloged into my memory. I'm standing, relaxing, breathing, waiting, his shoulder muscle contracts under the weight of my arm, he's ready. My heart starts racing. I make a silent prayer, "Lord, please help me." He placed the washcloth on the inside of my left knee then moved upward towards my thighs, he took his other hand and cupped my pussy with the base of his hand at my pelvis and his fingers touching my ass. I squatted a little to open my thighs accommodate the width of his hand. He continued with upward movements until he had gently washed the thigh and buttocks area, lifting, separating and feeling the weight of me in his hands. My breathing is deepening; my mind is working less while my body is working more. I noticed that he stopped moving. I opened my eyes to see what he was seeing, it was then that I realized my hips were rocking, back and forth in his hand, nature was winning, I was desperately trying feel the pressure of his strength against my skin, diligently working to release my fire. We locked eyes. In his eyes there was patience, minutes, hours, and days of patience. He continued to hold me there, probably trying to see if I was actually going to explode in his hand. I stopped and watched him watching me. As on impulse, he dipped, rinsed the cloth and began to rinse the buttocks and leg area of my left side.

He must have noticed the decreasing temperature of the water. He turned the faucet on, as he continued to add soap to the cloth. Keeping things in balance, I switched legs. He closed the faucet, switched hands, and continued the process of bathing, what seemed

112

at this moment to be, his most treasured possession. Minutes passed, everything has been cleaned, except my beautiful, full, and luscious vaginal lips. At this moment, I'm grateful for the bit of hair that I always leave to line the entrance. There's something about the magical feeling of moving the hair to separate the lips for cleaning or entry...

Just in case you haven't noticed, my brain is on minimal right now...

Ghost gets up retrieves a clean dry cloth from the counter, he goes to the sink, turns on the water, and begins to wet the cloth. I'm standing wide open like... hmm... 'hello?'

So, I ask, "You good?"

He replies, "Yes, I just thought you weren't supposed to get soap 'inside."

Fuck, all I heard was 'inside.' Heart racing, I stood there waiting.

He turns off the water, turns to the tub and walks toward me. I smile slightly, he comes closer, I keep expecting him to begin his kneeling ritual but he doesn't. He's standing chest to face with me. I had to look up to find his eyes. He motioned for me to stand with both legs on the side of the tub. I can't balance on the side of the tub with both legs, can I? Oh well, let's give it a try. Standing legs straight, alarm has registered in my face, and trying like hell not to fall. We start laughing. Demonstrating a bent knee squat, I'd imagine like a plié, he then asks "Can you stand like this?" Ok, Sir, you are officially tripping! Though, because he was trying desperately to fulfill my request, I obliged. He noticed that it was awkward, so he stood closer and instructed me to place my arms on his shoulders, allowing my body to lean forward.

Position achieved, he takes his cloth and began the daunting task of washing my vaginal area. He reaches down, gently spread the lips, first washing one side then the other. The cloth brushed my clitoris. I shuddered and bent my head into his chest. He obviously liked that response, so he brushed it again...on purpose. My response, shudder and moan. I'm holding on, my hands are locked behind his head, my forehead pressed into his shirt, this is the first time I've noticed his scent. Damn, I'm dizzy. I'm reminding myself to breath and hold on. He played there in that space, back and forth. My hips agreed and began to rock against his motion.

I could feel the blood racing from all over my body to try to connect with his hand. My mind? Relaxed. My arms? Relaxed. My mouth? Relaxed, so much so, that I can't close my lips and I can feel the increased saliva racing to escape its opening. My hips? Alert, ready to draw him in to wrap him all of my goodness.

I am slightly aware of the entry of his finger into the opening of my soul, two fingers, three. Damn. Hold on. With the base of his hand against the bone that houses my g-spot and the fingers penetrating my vagina, we are on one accord. My goal is to release this fire. His goal is to be the master of its release.

He wraps his other arm around my torso, drops the cloth in the water and places his hand under my butt connecting his hands, drawing me tighter, closer and applying more pressure to his other hand. Every blood cell and nerve in my body was screaming go, go, go and with that...an orgasmic eruption that took me from total control to please help me.

I'm not sure how long we stood there but when I finally tried to speak. I realize that I wasn't standing at all, Ghost was holding me, in a make shift cradle of his arms, hands and torso. He lowered me to the floor

114

and watched to see if I could stand. As I achieved that task, he pulled a towel and wrapped me in it. He looked at me completely, once more, then walked out of the bathroom and took a left into the front sitting area.

There I stood dazed, what just happened? I looked at me in the mirror, smiled slightly in amazement. Then I left the bathroom, turned right into the bedroom. I was listening, he didn't leave. What next? My mind was waking up. I dried off, applied lotion, slipped on a lazy dress...

I went to make a drink and seek my much obliging guest. He was sitting, having a drink, chilling. I looked at him, smiled and said, "Thank you for my bath." He said, "Yah, that shit was great." We laughed together. I made a drink, vodka with a squirt of both lemon and lime. Finally, the background music registered again. I started to move a little in its rhythm.

He excused himself to use the bathroom. I heard the text notification chime on his phone.

Me: "Would you like to come to bed with me?"

Ghost: "Yes."

I heard the shower come on. In true Joy fashion, I grabbed my drink and moved the music to bedroom. I removed my lazy dress, climbed into bed and waited... for Ghost.

Fairness:

*treating people in a way that does not favor
some over others*

We are slaying all the way to Jamaica Bitches!

I received an invitation to go on a girl's trip to an all-inclusive resort near Montego Bay. Denae' and I have traveled abroad together before; so, it was a no-brainer that she and I would room together on this trip of 12 or 13 ladies.

Traveling with Denae is like swimming in a warm pool with varying levels of depth. When I'm with her, whatever happens... happens. There's never any judgment. Hell, we may not ever discuss it again. We both have that amazing ability to forget some shit...

On our flight I announced to Denae', "Girl, I'm going to have a different husband for every night of our vacation." In true fashion, she replied, "That is a wonderful idea." Just like that, operation Jamaican husband-a-day was underway. Upon our arrival, I was giddy with excitement; the weather was intoxicating on its own but I had been drinking vodka before and during the flight, so my intoxication had a slight boost. Denae', on the other hand, was totally in charge, as she always is. Once we arrived in Montego Bay, I asked her as an afterthought, "Have 'WE' already planned transportation to the resort?" She laughed and said, "Yes, girl, come on." I shrugged my shoulders and followed behind her laughing ass.

Our shuttle to the resort was full. There was random chatter throughout the ride but, mainly, I looked out the window, desperately trying to catch glimpses of the culture. I looked around trying to see the faces of the citizens. I wanted to witness the lasting influences of the various island settlers. I tried to get my brain to adjust to being a passenger in a van that was riding on the opposite side of the road. Relax brain we have experienced this before. As I sat, I recalled a couple of similar situations. I was pretty much silent for the whole ride, just taking it all in. The sound of the radio interrupted my

118

thoughts, "What's that music?" "Is that R&B?" I asked, randomly, of anyone listening, "Where is the reggae?" No one answered. I slipped back into my silence and continued looking and watching. I could tell the city and streets were carved out of a tropical forest. The standing foliage was thick and dense; like a jungle, I suppose. The storefronts and homes were made of wood and some sort of painted clay of soft pastels. We passed various street marketers, selling fruit, jewelry and clothing, in a hurried blur. For the locals and the tourists, I supposed.

After an hour or so, the driver of the shuttle suddenly made a sharp right turn coming out of a curve. We stopped instantly. Startled, I grabbed the seat in front of me and looked up. What happened? We have arrived. We are at a gate. I asked, "Is that a security gate?" There were two shuttles ahead of us, filled with excited passengers, just like us, I'm sure. We waited. After each shuttle, cleared security, we moved forward slightly until it was our turn. Our driver presented his credentials, answered a few questions. Then off we went.

The first views of the resort were breathtaking. A beautiful island woman greeted us with smiles and some tropical drink, the name of the drink escapes me but it was yummy enough. Hell, I had two or three or four... I mean I'm in Jamaica, does quantity really matter? Hilarious! Ok, let me refocus... I understand the intention to lure the tourist and get that money but dayyumm! This place was beautiful. There were soft pinks, marble floors and columns, lush landscape and water everywhere! The fountains flowed into pools and the pools into the ocean. The bluest of blues as far as the eye could see. However, I want to be clear, to make sure there are no misunderstandings; the most beautiful sights thus far were the sights of the men working on the resort! The skin tones, the bodies and the smiles, my word! Can you imagine waking up sober in heaven and thanking God for the opportunity to be drunk in love instead? Have mercy.

Men were everywhere, working in all capacities. I know women across the globe will agree, there is nothing like a hardworking man. He can be working with his brain or his brawn... anything. As long as he is about the business of that moment, we all tingle a bit... Each of the workers flashed a dazzling white smile followed by "Welcome to Jamaica." I wondered briefly if the men in the city had the same brilliant smile and greeting... Hmm. I think not but if the universe is at work within me this weekend, I will find out. Aye, Jamaica!

Denae' and I are standing in line waiting to check in. Well, wait, Denae' is in line waiting to check in. I'm standing next to her but scanning the resort looking for husband #1. Not to mention I'm going back and forth to refill our glasses at the island greeter's bar. Seriously, I'm engrossed in real friend shit! I'm so not into the business of this trip, I hear Denae' say coolly "Hey Chick, put your wrist up here." I haven't a reason to question her command, so I lifted my right wrist. I felt the thin ribbon like bracelet slide around my wrist and pressure applied. As any kind woman would do, I turned toward the counter and saw the most beautiful man ever created. I was at a loss for words. All I wanted to say was "thank you" but for a few seconds, I stared and forced myself to breath. Then this thought hit me like a brick, down girl, this is a man-child. I immediately thought of my own growing women... I'm not that selfish. For a moment, I wished that they were here, that thought passed quickly. I took a deep breath, smiled and managed to say "Thank you." Of course, the attendant smiled and said, "Welcome to Jamaica."

At this point, I have sightings of three potential husbands, what if the chosen one says "no?" Hmm, I hadn't considered that before this moment. Oh well, we shall see. It's time for Denae' and I to head to our suite. We will take the shuttle because she chose a remote location close to the private beach. She is as much a loner as I am. Not to mention, we both like to wear as little clothing as possible. She knew that I would be cool with the location. One of the benefits of swimming in a pool of warm water, you never question the intention of the water, just flow with it. As we are walking to the shuttle, we aren't chatting much but we are in the same space. I'm still looking around, trying to put a wedding ring on this day. I made eye contact with a shuttle driver. I begin to walk directly over to him, I don't know if he's our driver or not but I was drawn to him. The closer I got the more we both smiled. I dropped my head and giggled a bit when I was directly in front of him. He said in the sweetest, most melodic tone, "Welcome." I returned his greeting with a smile. Then without prompting or thought, I introduced myself, "I'm Joy." He returned with his name, but yikes as I write this I have forgotten it, fuck it let's call him "Thursday."

Because I am who I am and true to my shit, I asked him "Thursday, I need a husband for today, will you marry me?" He looked at me, possibly trying to figure out what this American woman had on her mind, and smiled "Yes." He then looked at Denae' and back at me. I said, "This is my friend Denae.'" He greeted her. He said, "Dear, where are your bags? Let's go home." Ta Dah just like that... I had a husband. Thursday loaded our bags on the shuttle. I sat on the front seat next to him; as we rode to our suite, I placed my hand on his thigh. Why shouldn't I? He has nice thighs and of course, he is my husband. We talked about randomness. How long would we be here? Where are we from? Blah, blah, blah... I asked, "Honey, what time are you off?" He told me about 7pm. "How wonderful!" I added that I was looking forward to seeing him later. Upon arrival at our suite, Thursday unloaded our luggage and took it inside. He waited and watched us as we looked at everything. We were delighted at the raised Jacuzzi in the middle of the floor. He probably thought we were silly. I'm sure he had seen this suite a hundred times but whatever because it was our first time! The time had come for Thursday to leave, because remember, he was at work and I was at play. I reached up to hug him; he kissed my forehead and brushed his index finger across my nose. I blushed. As I looked at him, I thought, "God, this man is beautiful." We said good-bye and agreed to see each other later.

With Thursday gone, Denae' and I talked excitedly about what we would do next. Where would we go? Where are the other chicks that would be partying with us in Jamaica? We made comparisons to our current suite situation and the one we shared in Cancun a couple of years ago. Definitely some differences; though, both were lovely. We changed into our let's go the beach and drink outfits, which consisted of sundresses and flip-flops. Denae' wore a swimsuit under her dress. I'm ALWAYS naked under my sundresses. I don't even want to get in the ocean if I have on a swimsuit. Just seems so restricting, I would rather swim in a dress. We left our suite to tour the property, drinks in hand. Of course, we raided the mini-bar. Who wouldn't at an all-inclusive? As luck would have it, Thursday was making his shuttle rounds. I sat upfront with him again. Yes, I touched his thigh again; well, actually, I squeezed it a little. Just taking his pulse and I guess mine too. And boy, oh boy, was he alive. He just smiled and kept on driving. I wondered how he looked naked.

Thursday dropped us off at the main building on the resort. We tooled around until we found some vittles. We both decided it would be best if we ate. Great idea! I mean jeez... we are both women of a certain age and responsible enough, right? We ate in a fabulous dining room with a kinda buffet, kinda cook to order selection... Everything was delicious. After dinner, we ran into the rest of the "slay" crew. Now, the party shall officially begin, we decided to meet up at the room of one of the other ladies to talk, chill, drink and do that thang you do while you are in Jamaica Mon! We laughed into the wee hours of the morning. I had only two thoughts when I crawled into bed...first, this is going to be a fucking awesome trip and second, damn, my husband is gonna be upset with me because I missed our consummation.

Friday morning upon awakening, Denae' and I headed to get some breakfast. We walked instead of taking the shuttle. Let me tell you, just in case you don't know, I am a drinker, especially when I'm on vacation, I start my mornings with a cocktail, kind of a reminder that I'm on vacation. This morning is no different. When I left the suite, I had my first cocktail of the day in my hand. We chatted as we walked, mostly about last night's shenanigans with the ladies and the fact that we didn't have any hand towels in the suite. We laughed and talked and laughed. Another great reason to travel with Denae', the conversation is always light and easy.

Here we are in the dining room. I noticed two things, one was linen napkins on the tables, which in my mind equated to hand towels. I made a mental note to grab a couple on the way out of the restaurant. Hmph, then there was the bar set up with vodka and tomato juice for Bloody Mary's and another area set up for mimosas with champagne and orange juice. Lovely, I'm definitely going to enjoy this. As you would guess, I was quickly over the task of walking back and forth to the mimosa station, so I decided to bring the bottle of champagne to the table. Seriously, I'll never get tipsy with all this walking. Denae' just laughed and asked "Dang, you didn't get the vodka?" Hilarious, off I went on another covert mission to seize a bottle of vodka. As I'm trying to get up the nerve to pick up a bottle, I see my next husband. Friday is watching me; he knows that I'm about to commit a heist. It must be common at the Bloody Mary station. We maintain eye contact until I began to rethink my approach, then I lowered my eyes. Hell, I didn't want to get caught, it was my first full day here! What's the punishment for stealing a bottle of vodka at an all-inclusive? It that even a crime? I was trying to get my words together because I could feel his energy as he approached.

123

I'm looking down but holding my position. I see his shoes. I started giggling before I looked up because I imagined that I resembled a child who's been caught in some mischief. He said, "How may I help you?" I looked up, smiling brightly, and replied, "I'm fine, I have everything I need except..." He continued to look at me while waiting on me to complete my request. He raised his eyebrows to signal that I have his attention. I cleared my throat and continued "a husband." He looked with a slight smile. I kept talking, probably too quickly, to offer an explanation "I need a husband for today. I'm on vacation and my goal is to have a different husband each day." His smile brightened as he asked, "What do I have to do?" I said, "If you are my husband, anything you want." Laughing I added, "I'd imagine you'd do with me whatever you think is appropriate for your wife." His smile and the squint in his eyes indicated that he was actively thinking about what he wanted to do. Finally, he said, "Yes, I'll be your husband. I do." Just like that... I have another husband. We will call him Friday.

Friday and I made our formal introductions before we parted ways. I had to be considerate. Remember? He was at work and I was at play. As I turned to walk off, with a smile on my face and a spring in my step, I heard my husband say, "Love, you forgot your vodka." I smiled sheepishly and reached out to take it. I could hear him laughing as I walked away. When I approached the table, Denae' said, "Damn girl, what took you so long?" I held up the vodka with a tilt of my head, and said, "I had to steal this shit and not to mention I was getting married!" She started laughing. We poured our drinks and made a toast. "Cheers to us!"

We stayed in the dining room until we finished our bottles. Full and tipsy we headed back to the suite... Yes, I remembered the linen napkins... Denae' saw me. She knew what was up. She hurriedly exited because she was laughing loud as hell.

Well, Friday and I met up later in the day. I, of course, wanted some hoochie coochie playtime. This island ambiance had me feeling particularly amorous. However, my new husband had something else in mind. He showed up at the door of the suite with flowers and a beautiful smile. Completely caught off guard, I said, excitedly, "Hi Friday." He said, "Hi Beautiful." He asked if I could come outside to talk with him, while he was on break. I agreed to do so but I had to put on some clothes. I asked him to excuse me for just a moment, as I closed the door I watched his smile spread to his eyes. Inside, I hurriedly slipped into a sundress, brushed my teeth, put on some lip-gloss, shook my locks out and slipped on my flip-flops.

In my dramatic fashion, I announced at the door, "I'm ready." Friday turned to look at me. He walked over to where I was standing and gave an equally dramatic bow. I curtsied then accepted his hand. We laughed together and talked as we walked to another part of the property. His accent was heavy. I listened carefully. He told me about his family, various places he's traveled in the US and about living in Jamaica. I gave him my undivided attention. I was surprised that my mind didn't wander. We approached a wooden bench nestled in a garden area near one of the buildings. Friday brushed something off the seat and motioned for me to sit down. I sat. It was at this time that he handed me the flowers. I accepted and told him "Thank you." His gesture was genuine and very kind. He reached to touch my hand; he traced the lines in my palm while we talked for another 20 minutes or so. Then, unfortunately, Friday had to return to work. We walked hand in hand back to my suite. He bid a farewell until later... I stood on my tiptoes and kissed his cheek. We walked away in different directions. Smiling...

Well, well, well, I wasn't expecting that sweet moment. Friday, will make a great husband for someone one day. I gave a little smile and nod then proceeded to tuck that memory away in my brain. I'll think about it later, I'm sure. I changed into a sarong, no undies, of course. Now, I'm off to find the ladies. It's time to slay! It didn't take long for me to find them. Everyone was chilling together on a secluded area of the beach. There were beach towels and lounge chairs all draped by beautiful women. So, I added to the beautiful site, I grabbed a chaise lounge and a towel and proceeded to post up. This was the perfect location for us. We talked about everything from politics, to children, to men and all topics in between. We took turns making drink runs. The energy was crazy. We took many pictures. I believe this was the location of our one group photo. One rule applied to all though, NO social media postings. As I expected after a couple of hours, the energy became too much for me. I'm such a loner. So I said to Denae', "I'm overstimulated. I'm going to take a nap and reset." Like I said, nothing fazes Denae'. She said, "alright girl, I'll see you later." I said good-byes and blew farewell kisses into the air.

Back across the resort I walked, watching people, wondering about their stories. Enjoying the landscaping, how much is natural? How much of it was transplanted here for ambiance? My brain is always trying figure something out. I smiled at a couple of people, nodded hello and continued my stroll. Back at the suite, I ran a bath in the beautiful freestanding Jacuzzi. I noticed a supply of hand towels. I laughed to myself, housekeeping must have been like "What's with these napkins?" Either way they were gone. We didn't need them after all. I took a long easy bath. Candles lit, reggae music playing in the background from my iPad. As much as I am enjoying everyone, I do enjoy my alone time. I sat and soaked for a while. Finally, it's time to get out, I towel dry, and slip into bed naked. Sleep has taken over. I'm in Jamaica Mon.

I awoke late, I checked the clock, 11:11. I lifted my head to check Denae's bed. She was still out. I laid there for another minute trying to decide my next move. I called a couple of rooms looking for the crew. Found them. They were sitting on a balcony soaking in Jamaica. I willed myself out of bed to join them. I brushed my teeth, rubbed lotion on my body and slipped into a soft white cotton dress with lace sleeves. It was cute, comfortable and cool. Oops, I almost forgot to wet the lips... I'm rested. I feel much better. I hope that I'll be better company.

It was late so I decided to walk the street route instead of the sidewalk through the gardens. I had safety on the brain, probably because this was my first time here. As soon as I turned left onto the street, I heard someone say "hello." I looked around but my eyes failed me. The voice said "hello" again. I kept walking. It didn't sound like Thursday or Friday besides they knew my name. I heard movement in the grass behind me; I turned around quickly to assess the situation. There he was. Lord have mercy! He had a big gun. It was the first thing I noticed. Then I looked up at his face. I said, "Hello, you scared me. Am I under arrest?" He smiled and said, "Not yet." Well, secretly, I liked the sound of that but I just looked at him, waiting for him to explain the purpose for invading this quiet moment. He continued by saying that he noticed my friend and me last night while he was working. He wanted to meet us. "Oh ok, well, I'm Joy and her name is Denae'." He introduced himself, "Andre." He explained that he is one of the police on the property. He works the overnight shift. I nodded with feigned interest. I explained to him that I needed to leave; I was going to meet my girls for a nightcap. He, of course, said, "I'll be here all night. Can I see you when you get back?" I explained to him my husband situation and that I wasn't sure. He asked "What time does his day end?" I shrugged my shoulders, I hadn't really thought about that. Loyalty issues. Andre then says, "Well it's almost Saturday now." I said, "Yeah, I'm sure" considering it was 11:11 when I awoke. Andre wants to know if he can be my Saturday husband. I laughed and told him that I would let him know when I returned. He nodded and said ok, he would be waiting. Bye. Bye. I walked on.

127

I found the ladies, joined the rotation and sipped on a cocktail. Damn, Jamaica is everything. There were only about six of us in this moment, a few were asleep and the rest were at the resort nightclub. I was fucking chilling. I have no idea of the time when I left but I felt like I should've been walking into the sunrise. Was Denae' with me when I left? I can't remember. I had to have floated across the property in a trance because I don't recall taking a single step. I definitely don't recall the sound of my flip-flops on the asphalt. I'm sure I had a million thoughts but I can't remember a single one. The trees started talking to me, "Joy?" I responded, "Yes, what do you want?" I heard the voice again, "I've been waiting for you." Most natural response, "Here I am." The next words from the trees were, "Wait a second, I'm coming for you." I wasn't aware of any other options. I stopped and waited for the trees to come for me. I could hear movement, was it from the left, I looked. It sounds like it's coming from the right, wait, it's not there either. How long was I supposed to wait? Finally, I hear footsteps on the asphalt. I forced my eyes to focus while my brain remained unbothered. The voice was in front of me; wait, what did you do to the trees? He said, "It's Saturday." I agreed. "You are my wife today." I wanted to say, "No, you are my husband" but I couldn't find the words. So, instead I agreed. He took my hand and led me into the trees.

He was talking. I tried to focus on the sound of his voice. My eyes and mind focused on the darkness. I remember a lounge chair. I remember the stars and the moon was in waxing gibbous. I kept thinking it would be full tomorrow. I remember hearing his gun and artillery belt hit the ground. I remember him asking, "Are you comfortable?" I remember trying to separate the scents of the foliage from his maleness. I remember feeling his hands on my thighs and his teeth on my nipples. I remember moans escaping my mouth. Or was that his mouth? I remember thinking, are those leaves moving closer? How many stars are out there? I could hear the condom

128

wrapper tear. I remember the second before he entered me because he grabbed my neck with a force that made me open my eyes, inhale deeply and relax upon exhaling. I remember my hips moving to their own rhythm without any help from my mind. I remember trying to remember the last time a comet was close enough to the earth to see unaided. Wouldn't it be nice to see one now? Andre said, "You are my wife, cum for me." I held on tight, shifted my body and gave him what he demanded. I mean seriously, I couldn't afford to disappoint my husband on the morning of our consummation, right? I was lost in the moment but I noticed the sky becoming lighter, how is that so? Is that a comet? Oh damn, it was the sun. We noticed it about the same time. He finished his part of the consummation rites ceremony and proceeded to get up to redress. I fell asleep. I'm sure because I don't remember him getting dressed. I opened my eyes when I realized that he was trying to dress me. Now, we are both dressed and exiting the trees. He walked me to the sidewalk leading to the suite. I believe I looked at him but I'm sure I looked at the trees. I said goodbye to both.

I entered the suite, crawled into bed and slept... satiated.

"Rise and shine," sang Denae.' I opened one eye to check my location. I didn't dream at all there were just still shots of various situations. I completed my safety check by reaching under the cover, clothing: none, panties: check. I couldn't remember if I bathed when I got in this morning. I'll bathe again. I rolled over on my back and sat up in bed on my elbows. Am I balanced or not? I looked at Denae', her smile made me think of the sunshine, she looked radiant. Now that I think of it, I never told her how beautiful she looked. Her smile made me smile. I said, "Good morning Chick. You are ready! What's up?" She told me that the driver was taking us into the city to do some shopping and see some sites. "How awesome! How long do I have to get dressed?" She replied, "About 30 minutes. Meet us at the pick-up area." I nodded and then my brain registered that I had to move my body. I'm not sure that I can because it feels like it is still being held captive by the trees. Denae' grabbed her bag and left. I sat up some more and swung my legs off the bed. As soon as I stood, I was overwhelmed with thoughts from this morning. The moon will be full tonight. I managed to get to the toilet; I used it then turned on the shower. As I looked at my body in the mirror, I noticed two bruises on my neck. I touched them and my eyes closed. Damn. If I stayed in this moment, it would be an unproductive day. I made a cognitive effort to place those still shots with Friday's flowers; I'll process that all later. For right now, I must prepare for a day of shopping with the ladies in Jamaica Mon.

Twenty minutes later, I'm walking, cocktail in hand, to meet the ladies for Saturday fun. I said, loudly and kinda whimsically, "Hey everybody." I received and gave some hugs and kisses; we were all a part of this island moment. I joined the conversation as we waited for the others to get here. The driver should be here soon. I didn't ask the time; it didn't matter anymore. The van arrived, we climbed in and claimed a seat. We were all giddy with excitement because we are going into the city. We passed various shops along the way. We stopped at a roadside bar; there was a restaurant and a fishing pier attached. Before I exited the van, I noticed a lone angler on the dock. I was drawn to him. Interesting... So, in true Joy fashion, I went to the bar to refresh my drink then made a bee line to bask in this man's energy for a few minutes.

I walked up easy. I wasn't interested in disturbing his moment. I figured, if I felt him, he felt me too. I stood about a foot from him to his left. I watched him. He watched his line. After a few seconds, he lifted a blunt to his mouth and inhaled. Instinctively, I inhaled with him. He didn't even look at me he just reached across his body to offer the blunt. I remember there was silence, maybe a little music,

130

nah it was silent in our space. My mouth wanted to say, "No, thank you" but instead I stepped closer, and received his offering. I placed the blunt to my lips, closed my eyes and inhaled. He inhaled with me. I held the residuals of his gift in that space between here and there for a few seconds then exhaled. He exhaled with me. We stood there. Silence. I realized I was still holding the blunt, so did he because he turned to look at me. He watched as I placed the burning end between my teeth. He was ready. With great patience and detail, he propped his fishing reel against the railing and proceeded to kneel in front of me. I leaned in to his face, cupped his nose and mouth area with my hands and proceeded to fill his emptiness with the pieces of the universe that coursed through me combined with the residuals of his offerings. I truly believe that we could've stayed in this space forever. I stopped giving. We stayed in our space. With hands cupped close, the angler proceeded to inhale and nuzzle his nose in every part of my hands trying to inhale every piece of us. Inhaled, exhaled, opened my eyes and slowly removed my hands. He opened his eyes and stood. He took a deep breath and turned to check his line. I leaned on the railing of the dock. We are close. He smells as if he's been fishing all day with maybe a hint of soap. He smelled like a man. Neither of us said anything for a few moments, until he turned to me and said with a smile, "Welcome to Jamaica." I threw my head back and laughed loudly. Ha! They do say it in the city too... I returned his peace offering. I thanked him for his time. Farewell.

Back on the van, I sat, quietly, watching the city through the windows. Conversations were happening all around me, I was unable to participate. I was in a very low energy space. I was the only one in existence at the time. We made our last stop. I snapped a couple of pictures, sipped on a cocktail or two and purchased a couple of souvenirs. As everyone completed their shopping, I sat outside and watched the cars pass and the nightfall. I was at peace.

Once we arrived back at the resort, we went to the suite to put our purchases away then off to dinner. This Jamaica night was much like the others, consisting of laughter, friendship and love. I realized that we only had two more nights left on this fabulous vacation. This melancholy feeling settled over my mind and eyes. I told myself "It's too soon for that!" I shook it off. With that, I decided to go for a swim. I hadn't been since the day I baptized my dreads in the bay. Was that on Friday? I don't remember. It was late so the pool would have to do. I looked at my dress and decided it would have to do, as well. So, I went for a short swim. It didn't take long for me to realize that my body was tired. I walked back to the suite along the roadway. As I walked, I looked to the trees trying to remember exactly which one seduced me last night. I couldn't see anything but trees. It was crazy. I didn't see anything that I remembered but I did notice that the moon was full.

"Hey Beautiful." My mind immediately recognized the voice. "Andre?" He laughed and said "yes." I said, "Where are you?" I saw the flicker of his flashlight. I shook my head and laughed. He stepped out so that I could see him. There he stood with the trees as a backdrop. I reached up to touch my neck. He walked to me. I didn't move. When he got closer, I asked, "What's up with the cloak and dagger mysteriousness?" He laughed, "It's my job, I'm not supposed to be seen." I added, "Well, you are very good at it." He smiled. He looked at his watch and lifted my chin up to meet his eyes. I said, "Yes?" He said, "It's still Saturday, my day, right?" I took a deep breath and smiled with a nod and a shrug. Honestly, I had no idea of the time of day; but, what the fuck? Saturday was as good a day as any or probably better...

I asked, "Are we going to your tree-house?" He laughed and said, "If you want, though, I'd like to show you someplace else." Of course, I'm curious, so I say, "Hold on, let me grab a drink out of my room."

He said, "Cool." We walked to my room. I made a drink and realized that I wasn't sleepy anymore. Isn't it funny how that worked? Andre and I walked together in the opposite direction, after a little while I asked, "Are we walking to the private beach?" He didn't reply. We continued walking. Ha! The private beach, I knew it. Andre took my hand as we navigated the sand. I held on and stayed close. Finally, we stopped, he dusted off a chair and I sat down. He sat on a table next to me. We didn't really say anything for the longest time. I watched the sky. The moon was beautiful. The stars were bright. The ocean served as a mirror. I could see the lights of boats and ships in the distance. I had a strange thought, where are the animals? I can't say that I've seen any since I arrived at the resort. My mind is always working, oh my goodness!

It's dark as hell out here and quiet. We only have the moonlight. Andre broke the silence. He laughed. I looked at him, "What's funny?" He said, "I couldn't wait to see you this evening and now, I don't even know what to say." I chuckled, "Well, just see me then. Maybe words aren't required in this moment." He became silent again. I felt his hand feeling my thigh area. I guessed that he was looking for my hand. I placed my hand on his. He held it. Admittedly, I'm perplexed but I refused to say anything. We continued to sit in silence. I could feel Andre moving, shifting; I thought, "What is he doing?" All of a sudden, there was a light; not directly at my face but aimed to the side. Instinctively, my eyes followed the light but I noticed Andre was standing in front of me, looking at me. I refocused and met my husband's gaze. If I've learned anything in life, it's to hang back and allow men to do what they are going to do. Especially in moments like these. I didn't murmur a sound. Come on, Baby, let's see how this plays out. I'm here. I waited. He continued to see me; but that wasn't enough, he proceeded to reach up and trace the lines in my face with the fingers on his left hand. I didn't move until my eyes closed in submission and my lips required my tongue. I licked

133

my own lips. Silence. His fingers moved lightly tracing from the corner of my mouth to my neck. If I had to guess, he was drawing an outline for which to use in remembrance of our temporary union.

He was patient with his drawing. I was his ever-obliging muse. He moved lower, his thumb brushed my nipple. My back arched and both nipples responded by standing at attention. The right one was jealous but not for long. My breathing deepened. I opened my eyes to notice only the moonlight. Andre had turned off the flashlight and placed it wherever in an attempt to free his hands. I looked from the moon to his eyes. He was still seeing me. I let him. I thought about the time, fleetingly. As if he read my mind, he proceeded to let me know the time, because he pulled me to a standing position and lifted me up on the table where he was initially sitting. All the while, he was still seeing me. He turned his eyes away briefly, when he repositioned the chair directly in front of me on the table. No words. I waited. He stood between the chair and the table, my legs spread on cue to make room for him. He placed his hands on my thighs. Without thinking, I tried to press my heat into him. He held me firm. The pressure of his hands on my thighs prompted me to look down and then up. He leaned in to kiss me. Sweet, patient, wet, hungry, and seeking... I responded to all of it with a couple of nibbles of my own. I'm such a biter. He reached low to grab the hem of my dress in preparation to remove it. I let him. He then folded it for me to sit on upon the table. I thought, how considerate. Then I thought was that placed there to protect my ass or keep the table clean for the people eating their lunch out here tomorrow? Whatever, right?

Andre sat on the edge of the chair directly in front of me. He lifted my ass, pulled it to the edge of the table, spread my legs wider and began to bite my thighs and stoke my flames. It must have been pretty hot for him too because he dripped extra saliva on my clit. As it mixed with my own juices, I felt it flow down my vulva to my ass cheek and began to soak my dress. The sounds of the waves masked the sounds of him licking me, and as well as, my sounds of passion and appreciation. It is high tide? Or low tide? What time is high tide? At some point, my legs were lifted to his shoulders, his hands were holding my ass tight and close, I'd imagine like a watermelon. I know that's horribly stereotypical but that was my thought. My arms were gripping the side of the table providing an additional advantage for my hip action. I felt loud but the ocean responded even louder. "I'm cumming." My love sounds and cries washed away by the ocean coming to life. As the waves receded, I relaxed my arms and lay back against the table. Andre continued to hold me in the same position for several minutes. Until he repositioned one hand at the entrance of my vagina at which time, he inserted a finger or two inside. Simultaneously, he used his other hand to massage my lower abdomen gently pressing in and down, he wanted more. I could only lay there. He waited. Silence.

I opened my eyes to watch the moon. Andre was still stroking me with his fingers. I could feel myself responding to his attempt at awakening my oceans. I moved slightly. He stood. He was seeing me. I could tell. He leaned over me to touch my face, to see me better. I licked his fingers, one by one, instead. His head rolled back, his eyes closed, and a moan escaped his mouth. When I finished, he stood up. From my vantage, I couldn't see what he was doing but I recognized the sound of his belt and gun as it landed on the chair. I took a depth breath and tried to slow my heartbeat. There were a few more sounds that were unrecognizable then the condom wrapper, the process of putting it on, then his hands on my knees. He widened them and moved closer. I felt his dick brush against my thigh. Heat. I grabbed the sides of the table to brace myself. I can feel him begin the entry process. His hands are on my hips, he's entering blindly. I moaned. He stayed right there and moved back and forth and back and forth until my thighs and his hips and abdomen became one operational

135

unit. He rocked and I glided into him. We played in this moment for a while until it wasn't enough for either of us. He rocked back and forth harder. I met his thrusts with my own. He wasn't getting enough of me because I remember him pushing my knees further apart, pulling me closer and gripping my hips so tight. "Fuck", is all I could muster. All I could do was grind my hips into him, which signaled my control center to blow the fuck up. When he triggered, he let out a yell so violent and carnal that I was sure that it was heard from miles around. He collapsed into me, I stroked his head and listened to the ocean drown his sobs. It was dark. I never asked. I left the private beach before he did. It was Sunday.

Late Sunday morning, Denae's energy awakened the room. She's playing music and moving around starting her pre-packing ritual. I just laid there face down replaying the events from the previous night. As you already know, I tucked those thoughts away until later. I rolled over and looked at Denae's beaming ass. She just burst into laughter. "I've been trying to wake you for hours." I returned her laugh and covered my face with a pillow. "What's up girl?" She told me that one of the other ladies found a Captain who was going to take us out on his yacht in the early afternoon. Eyes squinted, I took in the fact that she was fully dressed. I asked, "Is it early afternoon?" She replied, "Yep, now, let's go!" I politely asked my mind to tell my body to get out of bed. It obliged. I took a deep breath and headed to the bathroom. Teeth, shower, lip gloss, sundress. Let's go...the only day of vacation that I left the suite empty handed. Ironically, as I was following Denae' to the docks, we took a right. I realized we were meeting on the private beach. I smiled a secret smile.

When we entered the beach, I looked around hoping to see any signs of our love making from the night before. I was looking for anything, footprints in the sand, a piece of the condom wrapper or resonating sounds of our moans. As nature would have it, traces of us were

136

washed away. I continued for a few moments to replay the scene in my mind. Refocus! I noticed that the ladies have commandeered a section of the private beach. Hey everyone! We exchanged greetings. Everyone was excited about going out on the yacht. Someone asked, "Where's your drink?" I smiled. Denae' asked, "Did you find your husband for Sunday?" I laughed and realized how tired I was. Reluctantly, I conceded, "It's the Sabbath, even God rested on Sunday." With that, my tone was set for the rest of the day. I chilled on the lounge chair. I chilled even more on the yacht. The scenery was breath taking, amazing, awe-inspiring all at once. My eyes have never experienced the shade of blue that flowed beneath us. My hands yearned to touch it. Can I feel the blue? I wondered how blue feels. I will have to create a new schema to accommodate this new finding. We pulled up to a make shift dock, our Captain chatted with a local. My eyes molested the homes. I knew that I shouldn't stare but I couldn't help it. They reminded me of a fishing village in Hong Kong. We watched the locals and they watched us. At times, I participated in the rotation and conversation; though, other times, I was lost in my own mind. Revisiting and processing my Jamaican experiences. There were only good memories to carry with me off the island.

Denae' announced that she would not sleep during her last night on the island. She's the night owl... I bid her an adieu and went to bed, which turned out to only be a nap. My world wind vacation has taken its toll. I undressed, showered again, climbed into bed and said "goodnight" to Jamaica. I awoke around 3am. True to her word, Denae' wasn't there. I laid there for a few minutes until I decided to venture outside to find her. For some reason, I was drawn to the first location where we all chilled when we arrived. There she was along with two of the other ladies. How in the hell are they looking so amazing at 3am? I joined in. "Hi ladies." They began to fill me in on the night's activities. We shifted from the chaise lounges to the

Balinese bed, prompting sleep to befall one of us. I have pledged to watch the sunrise with Denae.' I hoped to see that through. As luck would have it and thank goodness for my nap, I was able to spend that last morning watching my beautiful friend, Denae', as she watched the sunrise. Cheers to Jamaica Mon!

It's Monday. I'm officially prepared to process my separation anxiety. I'm always sad when I'm leaving or have to say goodbye. It's a part of me. I make connections and become completely engrossed in my surroundings. After breakfast, we are arranging a shuttle to pick up our luggage for our afternoon departure. Well, wait, Denae' is arranging a shuttle for our afternoon departure. Distracted by a beautiful smile and a giant laugh, I began to walk towards the owner of both. My mind immediately thought, "Where in the hell has this guy been all weekend?" He stood watching me while he was talking to another man. I recognized the uniform, shuttle drivers. I approached them both. "Hi, I'm Joy." I was talking to both of them but looking at only one. He stuck out his hand and introduced himself, Darvon, maybe. But, fuck it, let's call him Monday. I have a few hours left, right?

He asked if I needed a ride to our suite, I said, "Yes, we do." I went on to tell him that my friend was on her way. He said that he would wait. While, we were waiting I explained how I planned to have a husband everyday while I was on the island. He asked if I had a husband for today. I laughed and answered, "What a great question! Now, that you mention it, no I don't. Would you be interested?" He said "of course!" Denae' walked up, as we got in the shuttle, I introduced her to Monday. She started smiling and said hello. We talked about the island on the way to the suite. Before Monday left, he told me what time he would be back. He would come inside to get our luggage when he arrived. Excellent! I kissed his cheek, goodbye.

Now, Denae' and I are packing and jamming. We are sprinkling more of our goodness all over the suite. We have had an amazing time. Of course, we vowed to return to Jamaica. I finished packing first because Denae' packs a lot of stuff! I know she's laughing reading this. I went out to the deck to inhale the scents of the island before my departure. As, I'm sitting outside saying goodbye to my surroundings, there's a knock on the door. I didn't respond because Denae' is closer. I hear her call my name. I look inside. It's Thursday. Cute, he came to say goodbye. I went outside to talk to him. Can you guess who walks up? I'll be damned if it isn't Friday. How funny! Low and behold, here comes the shuttle, Monday is driving. I waved at him. It keeps getting better, out of the corner of my eye; I noticed movement from the right, Saturday. My insides are delighted. I couldn't have imagined such a more complete send off. I'm blushing from every angle. Monday comes to retrieve our luggage. Denae' walks out headed to the shuttle. She waves good-bye. I said aloud to no one in particular, "Look all of my husbands are in one place. How lucky am I?" Monday walks up behind me, prompting me to step forward. I looked over my shoulder and smiled. He said, "Yes, Dear, that is nice but today is my day, after you..."

He waited while I took a moment to say my good-byes and thanked everyone for an amazing vacation. Saturday stepped forward; he needed more than my words. We hugged and lingered in our memories. Monday said, "Now!" I laughed and thought, "Damn controlling ass husbands." I continued my smiled, tried to catch my breath and held back what felt like the beginning of tears. I talked myself into tucking this memory away until later. I'll unpack it at home.

As we rode off with Monday, I waved one last good-bye. I often wonder if each of my husbands shared with each other, what and how they shared with me. Farewell Jamaica, until next time...

Love:

*a feeling of strong or constant
affection for a person*

I remember thinking; I can't believe that I'm actually having lunch with Chance today. It's been almost 30 years. He was such a good guy when we dated. I wonder if he grew up to be a good man. He proclaimed his love for me with a promise ring. I wonder if it's still at my Mom's house, probably in her jewelry box? Those thoughts made me smile. We were so young, so idealistic, so in love. I'm sure neither of us even considered that time and/or distance would ever separate us. Well, as all young romances go, we were definitely separated by time and distance. However, on this day, that will all change. We are meeting at 11:30 for lunch. What will I wear? I need to polish my toes. We were about the same height then. I bet he's taller now. Should I wear heels or flats? I was causing myself to panic. I decided to chill. Hell it's summer, it's hot as fuck. I decided on wearing my shoulders bare, with a floral skirt and wedges. I can't lose in that outfit. Hell, I'm not going to lose at all, I'm meeting Chance.

I pulled up to the restaurant. Hmm I don't know what he's driving; Therefore, I can't look for his car. I'm cool with going in alone, so, I exit my car, grabbed my purse and straightened my clothes. I remember my hands lingering at my belly thinking I hope he's gained some weight too. Hilarious! Whatever, I'm ready. I proceeded to the entrance of the restaurant. If he's in here, he'll see me. If not, I'll see him when he gets here. As soon as walked in, I started scanning the lunch crowd looking for Chance. There he was. I didn't move. I couldn't move. I just smiled. I'm sure I must have looked as if the sunshine lived within me. Because that is exactly how I felt when I laid eyes on him. How exciting! He looked amazing. He was dressed well, conservative. He had a beard. His skin was clear and beautiful. I remember him being about my complexion; today, though, he appears to be lighter. Just maybe all of my years in the sunshine state browned me a tad bit.

142

He walked up to me. His smile was just as bright as I remembered. We were happy to see each other. This reunion will be good for both of us. We hugged. I grabbed his face and said, "Look at my Baby." He blushed. I had to contain myself. I wasn't sure if his colleagues frequented this place or not. I reigned in my elation. After a few moments of chatting, it was time to order. As I perused the menu, he said, "Everything here is pretty good but avoid the fish tacos they use an egg based batter." I smiled because he remembered my egg allergy. He was always so thoughtful and considerate. We sat at a corner table, which was great because we were going to be talking and catching up the whole time, after we ordered. The distractions and interruptions would be minimal. The waiter came to take our drink order. I'm always on go, so I ordered a margarita. Chance may have ordered the same, I don't remember.

Lunch was delicious. With our table cleared, we continued to sit and talk. Honestly, I wasn't ready to leave him. He didn't seem to be in much of a hurry either. When he asked if I wanted to go to a cigar bar, I was like "Yes, please." I relaxed a little knowing that our time together had been extended. I excused myself to the ladies' room before we moved on to our next destination. In the bathroom, I used the facilities and touched up my lip-gloss. I took a deep breath and smiled at the thought of Chance as an adult. He is a good man. I believe I even asked him that...

Upon exiting, I walked through the restaurant. I noticed him standing at the door waiting for me. His eyes smiled as I walked towards him. I returned the smile but added a blush. Chance opened the door and as I was passing through, he said, "I'll drive." I laughed and said, "Wonderful!" He led me to his car and opened the passenger side door. I slid in thinking "He's doing pretty darn well for himself. Nice." He went around to the driver's side. Remembering he's always had a sweet tooth, I started teasing him about his chewy fruit candies in the car. He laughed telling me how he still can't get enough of sweets and he loves red velvet cake. We laughed together.

When we arrived at the cigar bar, he opened my door and assisted with my exit from the car. I allowed him. I realized then that I was aware of him as a man in my space. We walked closely but we didn't hold hands. I wanted to touch him. I wanted to hold his hand, to feel my hand in his. Once inside the cigar bar, we perused the humidor and made our selections. We took great care to brush up against each other, as if by accident, in passing. I'm mild to medium. He's medium to full. At the counter, V-cut for me, straight cut for him. Torch. I followed him to a booth. It seems like we shared a common goal to sit in the middle of the bench. There wasn't any space between us. It didn't exist. We've been this close before, closer even. We were comfortable. I recall thinking this is the most natural feeling of my extended self.

We talked about everything including our families, our jobs, traveling abroad, and my upcoming plans to relocate. I remember feeling tightness in my throat when I thought about leaving him or losing contact again. He teased me about being so bossy. He told me a story about how I used to tell him that if he wasn't going to be on time when he came to see me, then he shouldn't come. I laughed and said, "Yeah, I'm still a stickler for my time." He reminded me of the person I was when we dated. So many of those traits that I've tried to cover or explain away over the years are intrinsically of me. He reminded me of me. We enjoyed each other. We moved closer. My leg crossed over his. He's relaxed. Where else should my leg be?

He shared a few photos of his safari in Kenya. He told me some fascinating stories from his travels. I could've listened to him talk forever. I wanted to listen to him forever. We puffed our cigars. I sipped wine. I can't remember what he ordered to drink. We

144

continued to talk. We didn't want to leave each other. I wanted to be with him on those safaris. I want to be with him on the next one. Hours passed, we realized that it was about 6:00pm. Wow, we've spent the whole day together. Crazy. Our mouths were preparing to say good-bye, our bodies said not yet. Chance started to rise to a standing position and reluctantly, I followed. We continued to converse as he took me back to my car. We said good-bye in the car. I was warm, encompassed by feelings of nostalgia and love, I leaned over to hug and kiss him. He hugged me back. Our lips touched, I opened mine to kiss him. He didn't return my kiss. It took me a second to realize what was happening. I apologized quickly, I shouldn't have done that. He, of course, said, "It's cool." I apologized again and said "goodbye." I opened the door for myself.

Driving home, I was flooded with emotions, good, bad and indifferent. So, my rational assessment was that I was happy that I could still feel love. I was thinking that I lost that ability. Feeling it with Chance was perfect because he knew me before all of the bullshit. I was grateful. I also decided that I wasn't sorry for trying to kiss him, it felt natural and it was what I wanted to do.

As reunions and meetings go, Chance and I promised to keep in touch. We were able to text and/or chat on a regular basis about random topics. I enjoyed the honesty in our conversations. I'd tell him about my corny ass dates. He would laugh and offer suggestions or comments. We were good. We were friends. One evening we were talking, he told me about a conference that he would attend in the upcoming months. He asked if I'd like to accompany him. Uh yeah, I love that city and with as much as I like to travel, I sure would join him. Cool.

I asked him about visiting me in November to attend a football game. He was like, "Let me check my schedule but I think I should be able to do that." He confirmed the next day. So, I would see him before the conference. Excellent. With plans in play, we begin to talk a little more. I'm not sure how the topic came up, it was probably initiated by me, about an expectation of sex during his visit. He was honest. He said that he didn't have any expectations for anything. He just wanted to chill and hang with 'his Joy.' I countered with "I have expectations that everything will happen." I wanted him to make love to me. We were always so sexually free. That's one of the sweetest memories I had about our time together. We didn't have any boundaries. I couldn't help but wonder what type of lover he was today. Oh well, we can chill for the weekend, no worries.

Our weekend approached quickly. I was fine though because I cordoned off a space for him in my mind, he and I were friends, life-long friends. I would certainly respect his wishes. I just hope my body can follow those orders. He and I decided that it would be better for me to stay at his suite to avoid driving back and forth across the city. Besides, I would be working on Friday after a long Thursday night of football. I remember packing my clothes for the weekend thinking, I'll pack my regular pajamas of leggings and a t-shirt. There was no need to sexy it up. Ha!

I wasn't aware of Chance having other plans for the weekend but I didn't want to infringe on his time or space. So, honestly, I only expected to stay Thursday night. I also explained to him that the guy I was seeing may ask me to go out at some point during the weekend. If that happened, then I would abandon him for a spell. He was cool with all of that. But in my mind, I knew that if that call came, I was sending it straight to voicemail. Too funny! I'm straight chilling with Chance as much as possible. Chance and I are good.

He has arrived and checked into his hotel. I'll see him as soon as I leave work. I was anxious, excited and nervous, all at the same damn time. I recall thinking this is what butterflies must feel like. I missed that feeling. Get it together Chick. Let's go have fun. I arrived at his hotel, parked, grabbed my hangered work dress and bag out of the trunk. I always giggle at the efficiency of my packing. I hate carrying stuff, so less is more. As I'm walking into the hotel, I realized that I had to pee so bad. While I was driving, Chance sent a text stating that he was downstairs at the bar for happy hour. Perfect! Bingo! I began to seek Chance's face as soon as the door opened. He saw me first. His energy drew me in. I saw him, the sun began to rise and the butterflies began the performance of a lifetime. Chance.

Damn, I still love him. We walked towards each other, he reached for my bag, and I said, in all of my eloquence, "Oh, I've gotta pee!" Hilarious. Real friend shit. He laughed and pointed to the sign for the restrooms. As I hurried off he said, "What are you drinking?" I replied over my shoulder, "Everything. Surprise me."

After I relieved myself and washed my hands, I returned to the bar. Now, we can hug officially. I couldn't wait to be lost in his arms, to smell him and feel his face against mine. Be still my heart. Hug over. We sat, sipped our beers and talked. We love to talk to each other. We talk about every fucking thing. Seriously, he is well versed in all areas. I believe this particular conversation was about Greenland and global warming. He proceeded to tell me about a documentary that he wanted to share with me about that very topic this weekend. I laughed. He is just as much a nerd as I am. I love it. We continued talking through a couple of beers and some trail mix. We weren't in any hurry; our time was our time. I mentioned that I needed to change clothes before we left for the game. We finished our last beer and headed for the elevators. I felt his hand on the small of my back as we walked. I kept his pace. I explained to him that parking at the stadium was horrific and that we should request a private car. He was good with that idea. He was easy. No stress.

147

Once in his suite, I hurriedly changed clothes. I asked from the back, "What time does the game start?" He said something like, "I believe 7 o'clock but take your time." I slowed my process. I needed to because my heart was racing like nobody's business. I took a couple of deep breaths to gain some balance. Once I finished dressing, I washed my face and brushed my teeth. I entered the sitting area. "I'm ready." I picked up my phone to request the car. I relayed the information, the car will be here in six minutes. We talked some more then left for the elevator. Again, his hand was on my back. I tried not to over process this, it's probably a habit for him when he's in the company of a woman. I just went with it. We left as soon as the car arrived. As expected, the traffic was crazy as we got close to the stadium. He knows that I'm adventurous and always in the moment; Therefore, I didn't hesitate to suggest, we should get out at the next light and walk the rest of the way. Chance is Chance, his reply, "Cool." He asked the driver to let us out after we crossed the light. He is such a thinker.

My favorite part of the evening was the pre-game surprise when soldiers parachuted out of airplanes over head. I was so turned up. The first jumper carried the local NFL team flag. The second had the U.S. flag. I could feel my tears of pride come to the surface. I love being a woman in this country. The last flag caused me to jump to my feet and cheer! Chance was like "What is it?" I could see black and splashes of white. For a moment, he thought it was our team flag. Now, he knew better than that! Later, we laughed at his wishful thinking. I shouted, "It's the POW flag." I was probably one out of 100 people standing and cheering. I turned to look at him; he was smiling at me. He watched me like my response was so natural, which it was. No judgement. I started to apologize as I sat down. He stopped me, "No need for that! It was exciting as hell. I just wish they would've had one more jumper with our flag." I rolled my eyes and said, "Right, like that will happen in this stadium." We laughed together.

Throughout the game, he explained various plays and penalties. He was talking from the player's perspective. He loves football. He went to college on a football scholarship. Or was it track? I'll have to ask him about that. One thing, I do know for sure is that he is still very athletic. He has definitely taken good care of himself. I remember looking at him and thinking, "Damn Chance, you grew up nice!" Ha! I may have even said that aloud. We had such a good time at the game. We stayed until the very end. Our team was victorious. Now, we have to find something to eat. We didn't appear to be in any hurry. We talked about food options. We laughed at the over the top fans. We joined in random conversations with people who passed by. Every restaurant was jam packed with sports fans. We finally settled on an ale house that was about a block away. Chance got the biggest laugh out of watching me try to find the ladies room. I'm sure the designer of this maze thought that putting the restroom sign over a door that wasn't the restroom was a great idea. Though, it had me all jacked up. If he reads this, he's going to laugh again, I'm sure.

Once seated, he ordered for us. I love when he orders for me. That is super-hot. He has always paid attention to the tiniest details. We enjoyed our respective meals and nibbled on each other's food just for a taste. Not to mention, we consumed a pitcher of margarita without any problems. Now, it's late, this bit of reality hit me like a brick, I was exhausted. We finished dinner and requested a car. It's time to return to his hotel. Funny, because there is no stress in this moment because we are both beat. It's been a long day. Sleep is near for both of us. Once at the hotel, I showered and dressed for bed. I asked Chance, "Is that a pull-out sofa?" He said, "Probably but I want to sleep with you." I looked at him with a raised an eyebrow, like "whatcha' talking 'bout boy?" He laughed and said, "Get in the bed. You are so silly." I shrugged my shoulders, like whatever and made an about face to head back into the bedroom. I climbed into bed and fell asleep immediately. I don't remember Chance coming to bed.

However, I do remember him taking my hand into his at some point in the night. My response was to find his leg with my foot. That is how we slept for the rest of the night. My alarm sounded. Time for work. He was about to get out of bed. I told him to stay put. "Rest easy, Sir. I'm good." He continued to lay there. As I was leaving, he said, "I'll find a liquor store to get us something to drink at some point today." I replayed his words, "get us, huh?" I guess I'll be back after work. So, I said, "I'll see you right after work. Later, Chance." He smiled and said "Later, my Joy." With that, I was gone!

My workday flew by, a fact for which I was super happy! As I was driving in that morning, I was thinking that maybe I should have taken the day off. Oh well, that thought is not of any help to me now. Knowing I was going to see Chance after work added a little spring to my step. I spoke with one of my girlfriend's, Natasha, after work. She and her husband were chilling at home tonight and wondered if Chance and I wanted to have dinner with them. I told her that I would ask him and get back to her. We ended our call. I called Chance to let him know that I was in route. I relayed to him the conversation between Natasha and me. I asked, "What do you think?" He, of course, said, "I'm good with that. Whatever you want." Cool. I sent her a text to let her know that we would be there in a couple of hours.

Once I arrived at the hotel, I hugged Chance. I missed him. He hugged me back and just looked into my eyes. I shook my head and said, without thinking "I can't believe how much I still fucking love you." The expression on his face reflected his surprise at my comment. I just looked at him, I didn't take it back. I meant that shit. So, whatever. Deal with it. As I started to push away from him, he held me tighter, which forced me to look back at him. We held each other's stare for an eternity or was it a few seconds. Hell, I didn't know the difference. He took a deep breath, exhaled and spoke, "I love you too." I believed him. He continued to talk, "When I saw you a couple

150

of months ago for lunch, I kept thinking, how is it that there is still love after all these years? Our love is true love." I smiled and agreed. We just stood there trying to figure out how all of this is still possible.

Alright, so I can't get caught in this moment, especially if I'm not going to give or get any hanky panky. So, I changed the energy of the moment by talking about my work day. He told me that he found a liquor store and proceeded to show me his loot, which included my favorite vodka, Tito's. This guy is too much. He also purchased some fancy smancy cherries, which I had to taste right then. He made us drinks and fed me cherries. I'll have to admit the cherries were delicious and rich. He added some along with the syrup to our vodka. Delicious! We talked more over our drinks. I told him about Natasha and her husband, Emilio. I asked if he remembered her because she was from my hometown. He didn't.

He's hungry. I'm hungry. We decided to head on over to Natasha's house. It didn't make sense to eat now, if we were having dinner with them. We didn't order a private car for this excursion, I drove. He was a good passenger. We listened to music, a little, but talked a lot. Our streams of conversations seemed to be endless. We arrived at Natasha's I explained to them that Chance and I were two friends who love each other. Moreover, that our relationship was purely platonic. They were like whatever; a friend of yours is a friend of ours. Just like that, our evening began. We had dinner at a popular pub style restaurant. Emilio drove. Chance and I sat in the back seat. Our hands found each other in the space between us, that's how we rode. Talking to others but holding on to each other.

I think our words of love knocked down a wall of uncertainty. Our hands played all through dinner. We talked through menu options. Chance ordered for us. I asked about drink specials. The waiter explained a happy hour, Long Island Ice Tea 2 for 1 special. He ordered those. I believe we each had two. By the time, we finished dinner Chance and I were both tipsy. Natasha and Emilio said they would make more drinks at home. I laughed as I was thinking, "Oh Lord more liquor." Now, there isn't any space between Chance and me in the backseat. The liquor has lowered our inhibitions. Empty space doesn't exist within us. When we were together, every void filled. Natasha suggested that we should spend the night because it was getting late and we would be drinking more. Emilio added that they have plenty of room. Now, I already know this because I have spent the night at their home on several occasions. They have to stop by the 24-hour store to pick up a few things. I asked Chance, if we should pick up toothbrushes and nightclothes. Since we hadn't planned to sleep over. He said, "Of course, cool, fine by me."

We all went our separate ways at the store. Chance and I met up at the toothbrushes. Our hands locked, we made our selections and headed to the check-out. Once we paid for our purchases, we sat on a bench to wait for Natasha and Emilio. Every part of us that could touch, touched. We continued to talk but closer and lower. We didn't want anyone to hear our words. I know for sure that it wasn't sexy talk, we don't do sexy talk. But whatever the topic we didn't want to share. Natasha and Emilio are in line. We watched them throughout their process then met them at the door. With everything loaded in the truck, I thanked Natasha for suggesting the sleepover. I couldn't have driven us back to the hotel. Chance agreed, great idea.

Back at the house, cocktails made and conversation ensued. We all had a wonderful time. Emilio and Chance were fast buddies. Natasha and I have been besties since grade school. We have many years of stories between the two of us. Eventually, it was time for bed. Chance and I would sleep in my favorite bed. The headboard is beautiful. It was hand carved around the close of the 19th Century. It stands about

8 feet tall. I, literally, have to hop up on it to get in or step on the step stool. Hopping up is way more fun though.

Upstairs, I announced to Chance that I was going to shower. It was either myself or the liquor that extended the invitation for him to join me. Well, whoever or whatever made the suggestion, Chance didn't join me. Oh well, sad face, sad face. We could have played naked in the shower, couldn't we? That was a fun thought. I completed my shower, dried off, applied lotion and dressed for bed. Lastly, I hopped up on the bed to snuggle in. At which time, Chance got up and went to the bathroom to shower. I dozed off. I felt him enter the room; I opened one eye to see him looking at me. I smiled and turned my head. I was caught trying to sneak a peek of a naked Chance. He got dressed and climbed into bed. Random thought, I should wash and dry our today clothes. We could wear them back to the hotel tomorrow.

Chance and I moved to the center of the bed where we slept all night. Throughout the night, we moved together, we couldn't stop touching. We held each other. We kissed with our noses. We breathed each other's breath. There wasn't anything overtly sexual about our moment. He laughed the next morning when I proudly announced that we awoke as virgins. We talked and played in the bed until late morning. He even had a fuck-it moment where he was about to give in to his desires, our desires. He said something like "Fuck it, it is what it is," which was my cue to halt that mission. I was like "Nah, it's not gonna happen like this." For whatever reason, he was struggling with the idea of us making love. I held him close to me and we lay in silence until the moment passed.

I'm not sure why Chance was reluctant to make love to me. I wasn't taking it personal. Whatever he decided, he would have to be responsible for everything that came along with his choice. I didn't give myself to him. I wouldn't give myself to him. He knows that I love him. He knows that I want him to make love to me. He would have to come to a resolution on his own. I would wait for him.

As if on cue, Natasha announced breakfast was ready. We collected ourselves and made our way downstairs to the dining room. Breakfast was yummy. I wouldn't have expected anything different. After breakfast, Chance and I prepared to leave. We had plans in the city. I retrieved our clothes from the dryer. We got dressed and gathered our items from last night's shopping trip. Emilio and Natasha told us that we were welcome to come back anytime.

We went back to his hotel and settled in for an afternoon of relaxation and us. We watched TV and talked. We are very comfortable in each other's space. Lazily we lounged on the couch. I believe we both dozed off at some point. It's hard to explain our time together. Like we could literally be nothing and still we are completely absorbed in the moment.

At my suggestion we made a move, I had some projects to complete for an event on Sunday. First, we stopped by a local club to vibe to some good music, enjoy a couple of cocktails and smoke cigars. I'm not sure how long we stayed there, it seemed like we were in a timeless vacuum. Second, we went to the hobby store to grab an item or two. Third, we had to print some pictures for a different project. As I was collecting these items, all I was thinking was "Damn, this is about to be a long night." Chance was chilling. No complaints. He was keeping me focused in all of the stores. He would say something like "Is that on the list or what are you using that for again?" "Why not get this one, you won't have to paint it?"

When we got back to the hotel, Chance left me in the business center to complete my projects. About 30 minutes later he stuck his head in

154

and said, "How's it going? I ordered pizza." Yep, I love him. Projects finished, I went to the suite. My drink was waiting on me, along with a slice of pizza. What the fuck am I gonna do with this man? I was full, tired and ready for bed. Neither of us wanted to go to bed because our time together would end in the morning. We tried to watch the documentary on Greenland, I fell asleep with about two minutes remaining. Chance nudged me gently to get up to go get in bed. The last thing that I remembered before I drifted off to sleep was him holding my hand. I woke up about 3:20am to get water. Well, the clock in the kitchen reflected 3:20am, my cell phone clock displayed 2:20am. What the fuck? It was daylight savings. I woke Chance. Babe, we have an extra hour to spend together, wake up. He looked at me while trying to collect his thoughts. I announced that I was going to the kitchen to get pizza, wings and make a drink. I asked him, "Would you like something?" He looked at me as if he wanted to say "hell no" but instead he just smiled and said, "No, thank you." I laughed and went to the kitchen. Well, of course, you know I brought my picnic to the bedroom. Chance sat up but he didn't eat anything. We talked about randomness, laughed and played a little game of nibble and lick for a couple of hours until we both feel asleep again.

As soon as I opened my eyes, I knew that it was time for me to leave Chance. I thought that I would feel some kind of way about this moment, but, I didn't. I mean, of course, I would have liked it to last longer but it couldn't. I knew that I would see him again. I felt comfort in his presence. I didn't feel empty as if I'd given myself away. I wasn't processing empty thoughts. In fact, I was full, overflowing actually. He filled me with his energy. I rolled over and curled into him. He wrapped his arms around me. He was aware of me in his space, just as I was aware of him in mine. I allowed myself a few more minutes to bask in his existence. I thanked him for all of the laughter and conversations. I thanked him for making time to come hang with me. I thanked him for staying true to himself and his own virtues.

Later in the day, he sent a text message to let me know that he made it home. Wonderful. He followed up with I'd like to come back in February. I smiled and replied, "I'd like that. Please do."

It was then I realized... I wanted to cook for him and feed him from my hands. I wanted to be the reason he thrived. I smiled to myself and thought "February, huh?" In my mind, I started planning the menu.

Postface:

*a brief article or note (as in explanation)
placed at the end of publication*

As I'm preparing to write this note, I feel my tears preparing to make an exit. Why? I guess I'm saddened by the closing of this experience. Maybe it's a mixture of sadness and elation...

Let's see. How shall I begin...

Tabitha? Real.

Lilli? Too real.

Kendall? The realest.

Denae'? The truth.

Natasha? Been real for years.

All of the men are real. Men are always real. Always.

Now, let me be clear, all of the names have been changed to protect the readers. I'm not worried about the characters, they are excellent. I just don't want people coming up to them saying... why didn't you tell me about this? Did you love her? What about me? Blah, blah, blah...

Dates, times and places were left out intentionally. Too funny!

The only fictional character is Joy. Kudos to her because she was brave enough to present as transparent. Her experiences, thoughts and emotions were put on display for your reading pleasure. Wouldn't that be amazing, if we could all just be ourselves? I mean without regard to society's standard of appropriateness? Or without the fear of being judged by a common man or woman? What if every morning we awoke to travel on our own journeys?

158

Hopefully, you were able to relate to Joy at some point during this portion of her journey. One of the most poignant observations for me, as the writer, was that Joy was growing as a woman, which was not intentional in the writings. Her actions reflected that she went from just being in situations to designing her own based on what she wanted. I believe that as women, we all struggle with the idea of being in control of our desires. We fear the stereotypes, the negative words and more so, that someone won't want us because of our stories. The brilliance in that thought process is the reverse, the person(s) who want us, will want us because of our stories.

As the creator of this character and writer of her story, I derived much pleasure in imagining the response of both men and women to her willingness to trust, be vulnerable, resilient and fearless. This experience has been cathartic. I have literally been able to remove some of clutter, just a little, from my brain. ☺ I have, also, developed a more advanced sense of self, independent of those by which I am surrounded.

Until later, the party in my brain continues...

April 2, 2017

P.S.   I'd love to hear from you soon. What's your story?
Email: joycelyn.wells@yahoo.com

References:

consultation of sources of information

Bible verses, retrieved from The Holy Bible (KJV)

Definitions, retrieved from *www.miriam-webster.com/dictionary*

Virtues, retrieved from *www.virtuesforlife.com/virtues-list/*

Made in the USA
Lexington, KY
25 October 2018